Praise for Beryl Bainbridge's

AN AWFULLY BIG ADVENTURE

"Wry, quirky, and macabre . . . Bainbridge's tough, pithy phrasing and her wicked eye for deceptions, evasions, and absurdities give the book a delectable, infernal energy."
—*San Francisco Chronicle*

"The strength of this novel lies in its realism, its clever prose, its faithfully drawn scenery, its memorable vignettes."
—*The New York Times Book Review*

"A compelling read, again demonstrating her acuity of observation and darkly comedic view of life."
—*Publishers Weekly*

"[Bainbridge's] disconcerting humor, her ability to establish character in the flick of a sentence, her clarity of style are all confidently employed in this impressive novel."
—*London Sunday Times*

ALSO BY BERYL BAINBRIDGE

AN AWFULLY BIG ADVENTURE

AN AWFULLY BIG ADVENTURE

A Novel

BERYL BAINBRIDGE

Carroll & Graf Publishers, Inc.
New York

Published by arrangement with HarperCollins Publishers.

First Carroll & Graf edition 1993
New edition 1995.

Carroll & Graf Publishers, Inc.
260 Fifth Avenue
New York, NY 10001

Library of Congress Cataloging-in-Publication Data

Bainbridge, Beryl, 1933–
    An awfully big adventure / Beryl Bainbridge.—1st Carroll & Graf
ed.
      p.   cm.
    ISBN 0-7867-0184-6
    1. Teenage girls—England—Liverpool—Fiction. 2. Actresses—
England—Liverpool—Fiction. 3. Liverpool (England)—Fiction.
I. Title.
PR6052.A3195A97   1993
823′.912—dc20   93-7980
                                                           CIP

Manufactured in the United States of America

Acknowledgments

Grateful acknowledgment is made to the Special Trustees of the Hospitals for Sick Children for their permission to quote from J. M. Barrie's *Peter Pan.*

The quotation from *Dangerous Corner* by J. B. Priestley is reprinted by permission of Peters Fraser and Dunlop.

Excerpt from "Burbank with a Baedecker: Bleistein with a Cigar" in *Collected Poems 1909–1962,* copyright 1936 by Harcourt Brace Jovanovich, Inc., copyright © 1964, 1963 by T. S. Eliot, reprinted by permission of the publisher.

For Yolanta & Derwent May

SLIGHTLY: *(Examining the fallen Wendy more minutely)* This is no bird; I think it must be a lady.

NIBS: *(Who would have preferred it to be a bird)* And Tootles has killed her.

CURLY: Now I see. Peter was bringing her to us. *(They wonder for what object)*

OMNES: *(Though everyone of them had wanted to take a shot at her)* Oh, Tootles!

TOOTLES: *(Gulping)* I did it. When ladies used to come to me in dreams I said: 'Pretty mother', but when she really came I shot her.

James Barrie, *Peter Pan,* Act Two.

0

WHEN THE FIRE CURTAIN HAD BEEN LOWERED
and the doors were at last closed, Meredith thought he
heard a child crying. He switched on the house lights,
but of course there was no one there. Some unfortunate
had left a teddy-bear perched on the tip-up seat in the
third row.

The girl was waiting for him in the property room. At
his approach she stepped backwards, as though afraid he
would strike her. He didn't look at her; he simply told her,
in that particular tone of voice which in the past he had
always used for other people, that he wasn't interested in
excuses and that in any case there were none that would
fit the bill.

'I was upset,' she protested. 'Anybody would be. It will
never happen again.'

They both heard a door opening on the floor above, and
footsteps as Rose clumped along the passage.

'If it was up to me,' he said, lowering his voice, 'you
wouldn't get the chance.'

'You're wrong,' the girl persisted. 'He was happy. He
kept saying "Well done". I'm not old enough to shoulder
the blame. Not all of it. I'm not the only one at fault.'

'Get out of my sight,' he said, and pushing past her strode up the corridor to waylay Rose.

'I was encouraged,' she shouted after him. 'Don't you forget that!'

He slashed the air with his hook.

'You don't want to be too hard on her,' Rose said. 'She's young.'

He followed her through the pass door and across the dark stage into the auditorium. When Rose saw the teddy-bear she picked it up by one ear and walked on with it dangling against the skirt of her black frock.

'Did you get through to the wife?' asked Meredith.

'I did,' Rose said. 'She's coming up on the milk train.'

He climbed the stone steps after her, ducking his head beneath the singing gas mantles until they reached the top floor and the round window overlooking the square. Only the fireman and the rat-catcher came this far.

'The note,' he enquired. 'Did it shed any illumination?'

'Who can tell?' she said. 'Bunny saw fit to put a match to it.'

At this hour the square was empty. The flower-sellers had long since gone home, leaving the orange boxes piled up beside the urinals. Between the jagged buildings the lights of ships jumped like sparks above the river.

They stood in silence, looking down into the darkness as though waiting for a curtain to rise. There was a sudden seep of orange light as the door of Brown's Café opened and the slattern in the gumboots staggered out to sling washing-up slops into the gutter.

Then the girl appeared from out of the side street and

began to run in the direction of the telephone box on the corner. Once she looked back and up at the window as though she knew she was observed. At this distance her face was a pale blur. A man with a white muffler wound about his throat rolled from the black shadows of Ice Warehouse and the girl stopped and spoke to him.

He fumbled in his pockets and handed her something. He was holding a bouquet of flowers in a twist of paper.

'The Board won't like it,' Meredith said. 'Rushworth is bound to kick up rough.'

'I'm a match for him,' said Rose. She was holding the teddy-bear to her sequinned breast, circling with the pad of her finger the cold button of its eye.

'I don't suppose,' 'Meredith asked her, 'that we can keep it out of the newspapers.'

'I could,' Rose told him, 'but I won't. The orphanage has rung twice already. God forgive us, but it'll be good for business.'

Directly below, where the branches of the lime trees bounced in the wind, sending the lamplight skeetering across the cobblestones, the man in the muffler stood relieving himself within the wrought-iron enclosure of the public urinal, one arm fastidiously raised above his head. They could see his boots, glossy under the street lamp, and that bedraggled fistful of winter daffodils . . .

1

AT FIRST IT HAD BEEN UNCLE VERNON'S AM-
bition, not Stella's. He thought he understood her; from
the moment she could toddle he had watched her lurching
towards the limelight. Stella herself had shown more cau-
tion. 'I'll not chase moonbeams,' she told him.

Still, she went along with the idea and for two years, on
a Friday after school, she ran down the hill to Hanover
Street and rode the lift in Crane Hall, up through the
showrooms of polished pianofortes where the blind men
fingered scales, until she reached the top floor and Mrs
Ackerley whose puckered mouth spat out 'How now
brown cow' behind the smoke screen of her Russian cigarettes.

She came home and shut herself in her bedroom off the
scullery and spouted speeches. She sat at the tea table and
dropped her cup to the saucer, spotting the good cloth
with tannic acid, wailing that it might be a poison that the
Friar Lawrence had administered. When Uncle Vernon
shouted at her she said she wasn't old enough to control
either her reflexes or her emotions. She had always had a
precise notion of what could be expected of her.

Lily had imagined that the girl was merely learning to

speak properly and was dismayed to hear it was called Dramatic Art. She fretted lest Stella build up hopes only to have them dashed.

Then Stella failed her mock school certificate and her teachers decided it wasn't worth while entering her for the real thing. Uncle Vernon went off to the school prepared to bluster, and returned convinced. They'd agreed she had the brains but not the application.

'That's good enough for me,' he told Lily. 'We both know it's useless reasoning with her.'

He made enquiries and pulled strings. After the letter came Stella spent four extra Saturday mornings at Crane Hall being coached by Mrs Ackerley in the telephone scene from the *Bill of Divorcement*. Mrs Ackerley, dubious about her accent, had thought a Lancashire drama more suitable, preferably a comedy; the girl was something of a clown.

Stella would have none of it. She was a mimic, she said, and sure enough she took off Mrs Ackerley's own smoky tone of voice to perfection. Admittedly she was a little young for the part, but, as she shrewdly observed, this would only stress her versatility. The audition was fixed for the third Monday in September.

Ten days before, over breakfast, she told Uncle Vernon she was having second thoughts.

'Get away with you,' he said. 'It's too late to change things now.' He wrote out a shopping list and gave her a ten-shilling note. Half an hour later when he came up into the dark hall, jingling the loose coppers in his pocket, he found her huddled on the stairs, one plump knee wedged between the banister rails. He was annoyed because she knew she wasn't supposed to hang about this part of the house, not unless she was in her good school uniform. She was staring at the damp patch that splodged the leaf-patterned wallpaper above the telephone.

He switched on the light and demanded to know what she was playing at. At this rate there'd be nothing left on Paddy's vegetable barrow but a bunch of mouldy carrots. Did she think this was any way to conduct a business?

She was in one of her moods and pretended to be lost in thought. He could have hit her. There was nothing of her mother in her face, save perhaps for the freckles on her cheek-bones.

'Carry on like this,' he said, not for the first time, 'and you'll end up behind the counter at Woolworth's.' It was foolish of him to goad her. It was not beyond her to run towards such employment in order to spite him.

'You push me too hard,' she said. 'You want reflected glory.'

He raised his arm then, but when she pushed past him with swimming eyes his world was drowned in tears.

He telephoned Harcourt and sought reassurance, in a round-about way. 'Three bottles of disinfectant,' he said, reading from the list in front of him. 'Four pounds of carbolic soap . . . one dozen candles . . . two dozen toilet rolls . . . George Lipman's put in a word with his sister. On Stella's behalf.'

' 'Fraid I can only manage a dozen,' Harcourt said. 'And they're shop-soiled.'

'Am I doing the right thing, I ask myself?'

'I don't see what else is open to her,' said Harcourt. 'Not if the school won't have her back.'

'Not *won't*,' corrected Vernon. 'It's more that they don't feel she'll gain any benefit from staying on. And you know Stella. Once her mind's made up . . .'

'Indeed I do,' said Harcourt. Although he had never met the girl he often remarked to his wife that he could take an exam on the subject, if pushed. His extensive knowledge of Stella was based on the regular progress reports provided by Vernon when making his monthly order for bathroom and wash-house supplies.

'She caused an uproar the other week,' confided Vernon, 'over the hoteliers' dinner dance: Lily got her hands on some parachute silk and took her to that dressmaker in Duke Street to be fitted for a frock. Come the night, with the damn thing hanging up on the back door to get rid of the creases, she refused to wear it. She was adamant. In the end none of us went. I expect you all wondered where we were.'

'We did,' lied Harcourt.

'She took exception to the sleeves. According to her they were too puffy. She said she wasn't going out looking as if her arms belonged to an all-in wrestler. I never saw her in it, but Lily said she was a picture. She's burgeoning, you know.'

'Is she?' Harcourt said, and thought briefly of his own daughter who, in comparison with Stella, often seemed an imitation of the real thing. He had no idea whether his daughter was burgeoning or not; night and day she walked with rounded shoulders, clutching a handbag to her chest.

'And how's the cough?' he asked. He listened to the faint scratching of Vernon's moustache as it brushed against the mouthpiece.

'No problem at all,' Vernon said. 'Absolutely none. Kind of you to ask. I'm much obliged to you,' and he ordered a new bucket and a tin of bath scourer before replacing the receiver.

He told Lily that Harcourt believed they were doing the best thing. She was chopping up a rabbit in the scullery. 'Harcourt thinks she was born for it,' he said.

Lily was unconvinced. 'People like us don't go to plays,' she said. 'Let alone act in them.'

'But she's not one of us, is she?' he retorted, and what answer was there to that?

*

They came down the steps as though walking a tightrope, Stella pointing her toes in borrowed shoes, Uncle Vernon leaning backwards, purple waistcoat bulging above the waistband of his trousers, one hand under her elbow, the other holding aloft a black umbrella against the rain.

It was a terrible waistcoat, made out of pieces of un-trimmed felt that Lily had bought at a salvage sale with the purpose of jollying up the cushions in the residents' lounge. She had meant to sew triangles, squares and stars on to the covers, only she hadn't got round to it.

'Leave me alone,' the girl said, shaking herself free. 'You're embarrassing me.'

'So,' Uncle Vernon said, 'what's new?' But his tone was good-humoured.

The three o'clock aeroplane, the one that climbed from Speke and circled the city on five-minute trips, had just bumped overhead. Alarmed at its passage the pigeons still swam above the cobblestones; all, that is, save the one-legged bird who hopped in the gutter, beak pecking at the rear mudguard of the taxi. It was such a dark day that the neon sign above the lintel of the door had been flashing on and off since breakfast; the puddles winked crimson. Later, after he had visited the house, Meredith said that only brothels went in for red lights.

Spat upon by the rain, Stella covered her head with her hands; she knew she was watched from an upstairs window. Earlier that morning Lily had sat her down at the kitchen table and subjected her to the curling tongs. The tongs, fading in mid-air from rust to dull blue, had snapped at the locks of her hair and furled them up tight against her skull. Then, released in fits and starts, the singed curls, sausage-shaped, flopped upon the tacked-on collar of her velvet frock.

'In the grave,' Stella had said, 'my hair and nails will continue to grow.'

Lily had pulled a face, although later she intended to repeat the remark for the benefit of the commercial traveller with the skin grafts. He, more than most, even if it was a bit close to the bone, would appreciate the observation. To her way of thinking it was yet another indication of the girl's cleverness, a further example, should one be needed, of her ferocious, if morbid, imagination.

Uncle Vernon paid off the cab right away. The arrangement had been struck the night before after a turbulent discussion in which Stella had declared she'd prefer to die rather than tip the driver. 'I'll go on the tram instead,' she said.

'It'll rain,' Uncle Vernon told her. 'You'll arrive messed up.'

She said she didn't care. There was something inside her, she intimated, that would become irretrievably sullied if she got involved with the business of tipping.

'You just give him sixpence,' Uncle Vernon had argued. 'Ninepence at the most. I can't see your difficulty.'

To which Stella had retorted that she found the whole transaction degrading. In her opinion it damaged the giver quite as much as the receiver.

'Well, don't tip him, you fool,' Uncle Vernon had countered. 'Just chuck the exact amount through the window and make a run for it.'

Debating anything with the girl was a lost cause. She constantly played to the gallery. No one was denying she could have had a better start in life, but then she wasn't unique in that respect and it was no excuse for wringing the last drop of drama out of the smallest incident. Emotions weren't like washing. There was no call to peg them out for all the world to view.

Mostly her behaviour smacked of manipulation, of opportunism. He'd known people like her in the army, people from working-class backgrounds, who'd read a few books and turned soft. If she had been a boy he'd have taken his belt to her, or at least the back of his hand.

All that costly nonsense of keeping the landing light burning into the small hours. Lily said it was because she remembered that business of the night lights—for God's sake, the child had been nine months old. He put it down to that poetry she was so fond of, all those rhymes and rhythms, those couplets of melancholy and madness that inflamed her imagination. Nor was he altogether sure she was afraid of the dark. Why, during the blackout, when the whole city was drowned in black ink, she had often gone out into the back yard and stood for an hour at a time, keening under the alder bush. And what about the time he had come home on leave and she had somehow slipped out of the shelter and he and the air-raid warden had found her crouched against the railings of the cemetery, clapping her hands together as the sugar warehouses on the Dock Road burst like paper bags and the sparks snapped like fire crackers against the sky?

She had always been perverse, had always, in regard to little things—things which normal people took in their stride—exhibited a degree of opposition that was downright absurd. He hadn't forgotten her histrionics following the removal of the half-basin on the landing. She had accused him of mutilating her past, of ripping out her memories. He'd had to bite on his tongue to stop himself from blurting out that in her case this was all to the good. There were worse things than the disappearance of basins. It had brought home to him how unreliable history was, in that the story, by definition, was always one-sided.

Nor would he forgive in a hurry the slap-stick scene resulting from the felling of the alder bush in the dismal back yard, when she had run from the basement door like a madwoman and flung herself between axe and bush. Ma

Tang from next door, believing he was murdering the girl, had shied seed potatoes at him from the wash-house roof. Ma Tang's father, who was put out to roost at dawn with his scant hair done up in a pigtail, had sent his grandson for the police.

The basin had been a liability. More than one lodger, returning late at night and caught short, had utilised it for a purpose not intended. As for the alder bush, a poor sick thing with blighted leaves, it was interfering with the drains. On both occasions, and there had been many others, Stella's face had betrayed an emotion so inappropriate, assumed an expression of such false sensibility, that it was almost comic. Perhaps it wasn't entirely assumed; there had been moments when he could have sworn she felt something.

For her part, Lily had tried to wheedle Stella into letting Uncle Vernon accompany her to the theatre. She implied it was no more than his due. If he hadn't known Rose Lipman's brother when they were boys growing up rough together in Everton, Stella wouldn't have got a look-in. And it wasn't as though he would be intrusive. He was a sensitive man; even that butcher in Hardman Street, who had palmed him off with the horsemeat, had recognised as much. He would just slope off up the road and wait for her, meekly, in Brown's Café.

'Meekly,' Stella had repeated, and given one of her laughs. She'd threatened to lock herself in her room if he insisted on going with her. Her door didn't boast such a thing as a lock, but her resolution was plain enough. She said she would rather pass up her chance altogether than go hand in hand towards it with Uncle Vernon. 'I'm not play-acting,' she assured him.

Stung, though she hadn't allowed him her hand for donkey's years, not since he had walked her backwards and forwards from the infant school on Mount Pleasant, he had rocked sideways in his wicker chair beside the kitchen range and proclaimed her selfish. A sufferer from the cold, even in summertime, he habitually parked himself so close to the fire that one leg of the chair was charred black. Lily said he had enough diamond patterns on his shins to go without socks. The moment would come, she warned him, when the chair would give up the ghost under his jiggling irritation and pitch him into the coals.

'Keep calm,' she advised, 'it's her age.'

'I'm forced to believe in heredity,' he fumed. 'She's a carbon copy of bloody Renée.' It wasn't true; the girl didn't resemble anyone they knew.

When he shoved Stella into the cab he hesitated before slamming the door. He was dressed in his good clothes and there was still time for her to undergo a change of heart. She stared straight ahead, looking righteous.

All the same, when the taxi, girdled by pigeons, swooshed from the curb she couldn't resist peeking out of the rear window to catch a last glimpse of him. He stood there under the mushroom of his gamp, exaggeratedly waving his hand to show he wished her well, and too late she blew him a grudging unseen kiss as the cab turned the corner and skidded across the tramlines into Catherine Street. She had got her own way but she didn't feel right. There's a price to pay for eveything, she thought.

Uncle Vernon went back indoors and began to hammer a large cup hook into the scullery door. Hearing the racket, Lily came running, demanding to know what he was doing. He was still wearing his tank beret and his best trousers. 'It's to hang things from, woman,' he said, viciously hammering the screw deeper into the wood, careless of the paint he was chipping off the door.

'Like what?' she said.

'Like tea towels,' he said. 'What did you think? Would you prefer it if I hung myself?'

Lily told him he needed his head examined.

2

THE JOURNEY INTO TOWN TOOK LESS THAN
ten minutes; it was a quarter past three by the Oyster Bar
clock when Stella arrived in Houghton Street. She jumped
out of the taxi and was through the stage door in an instant.
If she had given herself time to think, paused to thank the
driver or comb her hair, she might have run off in the
opposite direction and wasted her moment forever.

'Stella Bradshaw,' she told the door-keeper. 'The pro-
ducer expects me. My Uncle knows Miss Lipman.'

It came out wrong. All she had meant to say was that
she had an appointment with Meredith Potter. While she
was speaking, a thin man wearing a duffel coat, followed
by a stout man in mackintosh and galoshes, came round
the bend of the stairs. They would have swept out of the
door and left her high and dry if the doorman hadn't called
out. 'Mr Potter, sir. A young lady to see you.'

'Ah,' cried Meredith, and he pivoted on his heel and
stood there, the fist of his right hand pressed to his forehead. 'We're just off to tea,' he said, and frowned, as though
he'd been kept waiting for hours.

'I'm exactly on time,' Stella said. 'My appointment was

for 3.15.' When she got to know him better she realised he'd been hoping to avoid her.

'You'd better come through,' Meredith said, and walked away down the passage into a gloomy room that seemed to be a furniture depository.

The man in the galoshes was introduced as Bunny. He was the stage manager. Stella wasn't sure whether he was important or not; his mackintosh was filthy. He gave her a brief, sweet smile and after shaking her hand wiped his own on a khaki handkerchief.

In spite of the numerous chairs and the horsehair sofa set at right angles to the nursery fire-guard, there was nowhere to sit. The chairs climbed one upon the other, tipping the ceiling. A man's bicycle, its spokes warped and splashed with silver paint, lay upturned across the sofa. There was a curious smell in the room, a mixture of distemper, rabbit glue and damp clothing. Stella lounged against a cocktail cabinet whose glass frontage was engraved with the outline of a naked woman. I'm not going to be cowed, she thought. Not by nipples.

The stage manager perched himself on the brass rail of the fire-guard and stared transfixed at his galoshes. Meredith lit a cigarette and, flicking the spent match into a dark corner, closed his eyes. It was plain to Stella that neither man liked the look of her.

'Miss Lipman told me to come,' she said. 'I've not had any real experience, but I've got a gold medal awarded by the London Academy of Dramatic Art. And I've been on the wireless in *Children's Hour*. I used to travel by train to Manchester and when the American airmen got on at Burtonwood they unscrewed the lightbulbs in the carriages. Consequently I can do deep-South American and Chicago voices. There's a difference, you know. And my Irish accent is quite good. If I had a coconut I could imitate the sound of a runaway horse.'

'Unfortunately, I don't seem to have one about me,' said Meredith, and dropped ash onto the floor. Above his head, skew-whiff on a nail, hung the head of some animal with horns.

'Actually,' she amended, 'I've only got the certificate in gold lettering. They stopped making the medals on account of the war.'

'That damned war,' murmured Bunny.

'My teacher wanted me to do something from *Hobson's Choice* or *Love on the Dole,* but I've prepared the telephone bit from *The Bill of Divorcement* instead.'

'It's not a play that leaps instantly to the mind,' Meredith said.

'Hallo . . . hallo,' began Stella. She picked up a china vase from the shelf of the cocktail cabinet and held it to her ear.

'Everyone is always out when you most need them,' observed Bunny.

'Kindly tell his Lordship I wish to speak to him immediately,' Stella said. A dead moth fell out of the vase and stuck like a brooch to her collar. Meredith was undoing the toggles of his coat to reveal a bow tie and a pink ribbon from which dangled a monocle. Save for Mr Levy, who kept the philatelist shop in Hackins Hay, Stella had never known anyone who wore an eye-piece.

'Tell his Lordship . . .' she repeated, and faltered, for now Meredith had taken his watch from his vest pocket and was showing it to Bunny. 'It's tea-time,' he remarked. 'You'd better come along', and gripping Stella by the elbow he marched her back up the passage and thrust her out into the rain.

It was embarrassing walking the streets three-abreast. The pavements were narrow and choked with people and Meredith often slid away, dodging in an elaborate figure of eight in and out of the crowd. Stella wasn't used to courtesy and she misunderstood his attempts to shield her from the curb; she thought he was trying to lose her. Presently she fell behind, stumping doggedly along: up, down, one foot in the gutter. Meredith, the hood of his duffel coat pulled high, pranced like a monk ahead of her. She listened as he conducted an intense and private conversation, sometimes bellowing as he strained to be heard above the noise of the traffic. Someone or something had upset Bunny. He seemed to be in pain, or else despair.

'It's the hypocrisy I can't stand.'

'It always comes as a shock,' agreed Meredith.

'It hurts. My God, it hurts.'

'If you remember, I had a similar experience in Windsor.'

'My God, how it hurts.'

'You poor fellow,' shouted Meredith, as a woman trundling a pram, laden with firewood, prised them apart.

On the bomb site beside Reeces Restaurant a man in a sack lay wriggling in the dirt. His accomplice, dressed only in a singlet and a pair of ragged trousers, was binding the sack with chains. When he stood upright the blue tail of a tattooed dragon jumped on his biceps.

'I shall die under it,' said Bunny.

They had tea on the second floor of Fuller's Café. Mounting the stairs, Stella had started to cough, had discreetly wiped her lips on Lily's handkerchief and studied it, just in case it came away spotted with blood. She had known Meredith was watching. She could tell he was concerned by the urgent manner in which he propelled her through the door.

When Bunny removed his mackintosh the belt swung out and tipped over the milk jug on the table nearest to the hat stand. The pink cloth was so boldly starched the milk wobbled in a tight globule beside the sugar bowl. Bunny didn't notice. The occupants of the table, three elderly ladies hung with damp fox furs, apologised.

Stella said she needed to keep her coat on.

'You're drenched,' protested Meredith.

'It's not important,' she said. Dressing that morning neither she nor Lily had bargained on her frock being seen. It was her best frock, her party frock, but the velvet attracted the dust. Time enough to buy new clothes, Lily had said, when and if she got the job.

As Meredith advanced between the tables a little shiver of excitement disturbed the room. The women, the afternoon shoppers, recognised him. There was a hitching of veils, a snapping of handbags as they slipped out powder compacts and began to titivate; pretending not to notice, they were all eyes. The manageress made a point of coming over to explain there had been a run on confectioneries. She boasted she was in control of two Eccles cakes. Mr Potter had only to say the word and they were his. 'How very kind,' he murmured.

'I'm not hungry,' said Stella, and stared into the distance as though she glimpsed things not visible to other people. Almost immediately she adjusted her lips into a half smile; often when she thought she was looking soulful Uncle Vernon accused her of sullenness. She felt ill at ease and put it down to Meredith's monocle. One eye monstrously enlarged, he was studying the wall beyond her left shoulder. She tried to say something, but her tongue wouldn't move. It was disconcerting to be struck dumb. Ever since she could remember she had chatted to Lily's lodgers. Most of them had spoken dully of their homes, of the twin beds with matching valances; the sort of vegetables that grew best on their allotments. They had flourished hazy snapshots of wives with plucked eyebrows, of small children in striped bathing costumes messing about in rock pools. A few, in drink, had overstepped the mark and attempted to kiss her; one had succeeded, in the hall when she was pulling the dead leaves off the aspidistra. Though she had made a face and afterwards scrubbed her mouth on the roller towel, she hadn't minded. None of them had ignored her.

'How can I shut my eyes to it?' moaned Bunny. 'Disloyalty is unforgivable.'

'I don't agree,' said Meredith. 'There are worse things. Malice, for instance.' The monocle jumped from the bone of his brow and bounced against his shirt front.

'I know a man,' Stella said, 'who never closes his eyes. He can't, not even when he's asleep. His aeroplane crash-landed in Holland and his face caught fire. They peeled skin from his shoulders to fashion new eyelids, but they didn't work.' She opened her own eyes wide and stopped blinking.

'How interesting,' said Meredith.

'When his sweetheart came to visit him she threw him over and omitted to return the ring. Afterwards she sent him a letter saying she knew she was a bad lot but she was afraid the eyelids would get passed on to the children. He says the worst thing is people thinking he looks fierce when most days he's weeping inside.'

'Oh hell,' Bunny said. Scales of Eccles cake drifted from his shocked mouth.

Meredith appeared to be listening, but Stella could tell his mind was wandering. She had the curious feeling she reminded him of someone else, someone he couldn't put a name to. Earlier she had thought him insipid: his complexion too fair, his expression too bland. He had taken so little notice of her that she suspected he was perceptive only about himself. Now, in the slight flaring of his nostrils, the disdainful slant of his head, she saw that he judged her naive. But for the discoloration of those tapering, nicotine-stained fingers drumming the tablecloth, she might have been afraid of him.

For a moment she considered giving way to another fit of coughing; instead she began to tell him about Lily and Uncle Vernon and the Aber House Hotel. She had nothing to lose. It was obvious he wasn't going to give her the opportunity to recite her set piece from *The Bill of Divorcement*.

She admitted it wasn't exactly an hotel, more of a boarding-house really, in spite of the new bath Uncle Vernon had installed two years ago. The sign had flickered over the door when Lily bought the house, and as the hotel was already known by that name in the trade it would have been foolish to change it. Lily had painted the window-frames and door cream, but the travellers walked past, bemused at the alteration, and Uncle Vernon reverted to red. Lily thought it looked garish. Originally Lily and her sister Renée had intended to run the business together, only Renée soon put the kibosh on the intention by skedaddling off to London. She wasn't a great loss to the enterprise. Nobody denied she had style, but who needed style in a back street in Liverpool? The travellers, faced with those pictures in the hall, those taffeta cushions squashed against the bed heads, began to drop away. Several regulars, including the soap man with one arm and the cork salesman with the glass eye, were seen lugging suitcases of samples into Ma Tang's next door.

'What sort of pictures?' enquired Bunny.

'Engravings,' Stella said, 'of damsels in distress with nothing on, tied to trees without any explanation. Besides, her voice got on their nerves. It was too ladylike. She came back once and it was a mistake. After that trouble with the night lights, when the neighbours reported her, her days were numbered.'

'What did the neighbours report her for?' asked Bunny. He wasn't the only one intrigued by the conversation. The women at the next table were sitting bolt upright, heads cocked.

'Things,' Stella said. 'Things I can't divulge.' She looked at Meredith and caught him yawning. 'Later on, Uncle Vernon stepped into the breach. He's the power behind the throne. He says I'll do least harm if I'm allowed to go on the stage.'

Bunny professed to like the sound of Uncle Vernon. He said he was evidently a man of hidden depths and it was clear Stella took after him rather than her mother.

'Oh, but you're wrong,' she protested. 'It must be my mother, for Uncle Vernon's nothing to me.'

Meredith was still yawning. There was a glint of gold metal in his back teeth as he took a ten-shilling note out of his wallet and waved it at the waitress.

Excusing herself, Stella went to the ladies' room where she made a show of washing her hands. In the mirror she could see the reflection of the attendant, red curls trapped in a silvery snood, slumped dozing on an upright chair beside the toilet door. There was no more than five pence in the pink saucer on the vanity table. It was not enough to pay for a share in a pot of tea for three, not with a tip and two cakes, and how could she slide it into her pocket without being heard?

Which was better, Meredith taking her for a gold-digger, or being arrested for theft? She supposed she could faint. Mrs Ackerley had taught her how to make her muscles go limp, and to act a wardrobe. Meredith was hardly likely to demand a contribution to the bill if she was laid out on the floor. But then she might fall awkwardly, exposing her suspender tops like a street-walker. I'm my own worst enemy, she thought. Uncle Vernon had offered her money but she had turned up her nose.

She managed to slip three pennies up her sleeve, heart thumping, before she lost her nerve and trailed out into the café to find the two men, coats on, waiting for her by the exit.

In the street Meredith said they would meet again when the season started. Bunny would be in charge of her. 'But you've not seen me act,' she said, startled; already she had reconciled herself to a career at Woolworth's. He raised his eyebrows and said he rather thought he had. He told her the theatre secretary would be in touch in due course. She blushed when he shook her hand.

'I look forward to meeting you again,' said Bunny gallantly. He kissed her cheek and offered to hail a taxi.

'I've some shopping to do,' she said. 'I'll pick one up later. Uncle Vernon never travels by cab because he finds tipping degrading. Isn't that foolish? Thank you very much for the tea.'

It was no longer raining, and patches of cold sunlight punctured the clouds. She ran over the road as though she had just spotted someone important to her, and continued to race half way up Bold Street before stopping to look back. A tram, impeded by a coal cart, blocked her view; yet when it had rattled on she imagined she spied Meredith, hood pulled over his head, striding along Hanover Place in the direction of the river. Deep down she knew it wasn't him. For the rest of my life, she thought, I shall glimpse you in crowds.

She walked on up the hill towards St Luke's where she fancied her grandfather had once played the organ. There were purple weeds blowing through the stonework of the smashed tower hanging in giddy steps beneath the sky. Uncle Vernon called it an eyesore; he couldn't see why the corporation didn't demolish the whole edifice and finish off what the Luftwaffe had begun. She'd argued that the church was a monument, that the shattered tower was a ladder climbing from the past to the future.

Now she realised the past didn't count and that her future had nothing to do with broken masonry. Love, she told herself, would be her staircase to the stars and, moved as she was by the grand ring to the sentiment, tears squeezed into her eyes.

At the top of the hill, on the corner by the Commercial Hotel, she telephoned mother, using the three pennies pinched from the saucer in Fuller's Café. The sun was already beginning to set, bruising the sky above the Golden Dragon.

'I don't feel guilty,' she confided. 'There are some actions which are expedient, wouldn't you agree? Besides, nobody saw me.'

Mother said the usual things.

3

THE STAGE WAS SO POORLY LIT IT WAS IMPOS-
sible to see into the corners. The fire curtain had been
lowered in an attempt to keep the worst of the dust from
the auditorium. A solitary man sat astride a paint be-
spattered bench sawing a length of wood. When he shoved
his arm the shadow of his saw raced ahead and broke off
like a blade. Geoffrey and Stella spoke in whispers, as
though in church.

'It's deeper than I expected,' Geoffrey said.

'And muckier,' said Stella who, left to herself, might
have conjured a blasted heath out of the darkness, an air-
craft hangar, an operatic, book-furnished study in which
Faustus could sell his soul to the Devil. She was distracted
by Geoffrey who was trying to tug a lock of his hair down
over his forehead. It was one of his mannerisms. His hair,
being coarse and crinkly, sprang back the moment he let
go. Almost at once Stella tiptoed to the back of the stage
and returned through the sliding door to the prop room.
Geoffrey was a thorn in the flesh.

She had thought when she was summoned to work in
the theatre that she was one of a chosen few. Finding
Geoffrey included in the roll-call of honour shook her

illusions. He was nineteen, three years older than herself.
A nephew of Rushworth, chairman of the governing board,
he had recently left a military academy after firing a gun
at someone he wasn't supposed to.

Geoffrey and Stella were both called students. George,
the property master, said they were really assistant stage
managers, but this way it meant the theatre didn't have to
pay them. Geoffrey wore a paisley cravat and walked with
his hands clenched into fists as though he still strutted a
parade ground. He kept throwing up words whose meaning Stella more or less understood but would never have
had the nerve to thread into a conversation. She was shaky
on pronunciation.

For instance, button-holing Bunny, whose eyelids quiv-
ered with boredom, Geoffrey said that in his opinion T.S.
Eliot was a poet *manqué*. He went so far as to recite several
obscure lines:

> Declines. On the Rialto once.
> The rats are underneath the piles.
> The Jew is underneath the lot.
> Money in furs. The boatman smiles . . .

It was a rum quotation. Of course Stella knew he wasn't
referring to the Rialto cinema on Upper Parliament Street,
but she couldn't help smiling. Uncle Vernon had piles.

Geoffrey went even further and said that any man who
squandered his energies on behalf of a Bank was incapable,
a priori, of speaking with authority. Stella wondered
whether Geoffrey was anti-Semitic. No one but a bigot,

after what had happened, would lump rats and Jews together.

It was odd Geoffrey sounding clever on account of words when in other respects he was clearly pig-ignorant. If George addressed him directly, face to face, Geoffrey stepped backwards with his chin in the air like a girl taking umbrage. When George brewed up the tea and handed it round, Geoffrey wiped the rim of the mug with his handkerchief, and sometimes the handle. He didn't care if George saw him. Nor had he an ounce of curiosity. Stella had coughed on and off for half an hour in the snack-bar of the News Theatre in Clayton Square and he hadn't once asked her if she was in line for consumption.

All the same he threw her off balance. Uncle Vernon had always given her to understand she was brighter than most. His business acquaintance, Mr Harcourt, an old boy of the Liverpool Collegiate in spite of landing up in toilet rolls, had backed his assumption. But for George she might have sunk under the weight of her new-found ignorance.

It was George rather than Bunny who took charge of her. Bunny was there, padding up and down the stone passages in his galoshes, but he was too occupied to pay her and Geoffrey much attention. It was left to George to explain that Meredith was away in London with the set designer, choosing costumes for the opening production. Until then, in the hope that Meredith would stumble across her, Stella had wasted the best part of three days hunched on the stairs turning over the pages of a library edition of Shakespeare's tragedies. She had combed her hair so often in anticipation she imagined it had grown thinner.

It was George who informed her that the actors wouldn't be arriving for another ten days. One or two of the junior members might sidle in to enquire about digs, but she needn't expect to spot Richard St Ives, the leading man, or Dorothy Blundell, his opposite number, until the very last moment. St Ives and Miss Blundell, along with Babs Osborne, the character juvenile, had been in last season's company. It was unusual in repertory to be engaged for a second term, although before the war P.L. O'Hara, by public demand, had returned three years running. Not that St Ives could hold a candle to P.L. O'Hara. Had he wanted, and the hostilities not intervened, O'Hara might have come back for a fourth season.

'What's a character juvenile?' asked Stella, and George said it was any girl not handsome enough to be a straight juvenile. He didn't look her in the eye, but she wasn't offended; she had always known to which category she belonged.

St Ives and Dorothy Blundell shared the same digs, though there was nothing going on between them. Since playing the Queen to his King in the 1938 production of *Richard II,* Miss Blundell had carried a torch for P.L. O'Hara. She was wasting her time. In life, as in the play, she had never been more than an appendage. According to George, Dotty Blundell was an unrequited woman.

St Ives preferred to woo touring actresses appearing at the Royal Court or the Empire. Having loved them, it was convenient the way they left him. Last year he'd clicked with the lead in *Rose Marie,* a soprano with legs that wouldn't have disgraced a piano stool and twin infants being bottle-fed by her Mum in Blackburn.

'I saw it,' cried Stella, greatly excited, remembering Lily's birthday treat, and Uncle Vernon turning queasy in the second interval following high tea in the Golden Dragon.

'Rose Marie' had misunderstood St Ives's intentions. Her tour had moved on to the Hippodrome in Leeds and on the Sunday, starting at dawn and driven by a trombonist in the orchestra who was sweet on her, she had motored all the way back to Liverpool. The trombone player, thinking they'd returned to collect a ration book left with the landlady, had remained outside in Faulkner Square, puffing on a cigar. He'd wound up the window when the bells of the Anglican cathedral began to ring for morning service and missed altogether the commotion inside the boarding-house. The penny having dropped—St Ives and a woman he swore was his Auntie from Cardiff were discovered in matching pyjamas, he in the top and she in the bottoms— 'Rose Marie' took a screwdriver, normally used to poke the fat from the gas jets on the cooker, and attempted to stab him in the groin. St Ives had got into hot water over it with Rose Lipman; she'd said he could have gone down with blood poisoning and jeopardised the season. Babs Osborne was the paramour of a Polish ex-fighter pilot who was now big in scrap metal.

'He's romancing,' said Geoffrey. 'I've met his sort before. He's just trying to make out he's pally with them all.'

'The cooker bit sounds authentic,' argued Stella. 'You don't mention fat for nothing.'

She felt at ease with George. He had lent her a dark blue overall to guard her clothes from the dust. It covered almost completely the mustard-coloured slacks and jumper that Lily had bought her. Once, running back across the square from Brown's café with a fried-egg sandwich for Bunny, she had bumped into Uncle Vernon. He had been to St John's market to buy a lump of pork and looked beaten.

'What are you got up like that for?' he had demanded, outraged at her appearance.

'It's a sort of uniform,' she said. 'It's obligatory.'

The next day, seeing her dressed in such workmanlike attire, Bunny had disconcertingly handed her a measuring rule and a stub of chalk and instructed her to work out the dimensions of a door, stage right, which would feature on the set of *Dangerous Corner*. He had talked mysteriously of an angle of forty-five degrees. Half an hour later, returning to the wings and finding the boards unmarked, he had sought Stella out in the prop room. She was making a great show of sand-papering the wheels of the bicycle perched on the sofa. 'Anything wrong?' he said. He was very pale and his lips looked swollen.

'I don't know what you mean about dimensions,' she said.

'What particular bit defeats you?' he asked patiently.

'All of it,' she admitted. 'I've never got the hang of feet and inches.' She knew by his expression, the clamp of his dry mouth, that he was annoyed. 'I'm not being awkward,' she said. 'It's just that I had a disturbed schooling.'

'Think nothing of it,' he retorted, and sent her upstairs

to fetch Geoffrey down from the paint-frame. Geoffrey laid a newspaper on the stage to protect the knees of his cavalry-twill trousers and finished the task in two minutes flat.

'It's not that I thought the job demeaning,' Stella assured George. 'Uncle Vernon says I haven't the humility to find anything beneath me.'

There and then George made her measure the rail of the fire-guard. Twice the rule snapped back and drew blood. 'There must be a better way of learning something,' whined Stella, sucking her fingers. 'Get away,' said George, whose own knowledge of such things had been acquired through pain.

At fourteen he had gone straight from St Aloysius's school to shift scenery at the Royal Court. If he slopped whitewash onto the floor the stage manager clouted him over the ear with the brush and, if he forgot to grease the rag in which the tools were rolled, at curtain fall he had sixpence docked from his wages. When he cut short a length of timber the master carpenter brought the saw down on his knuckles.

Having learnt all he could, George had given in his notice and applied up the road to the Repertory Company. His very first job had been in that celebrated production of *Richard II* in which P.L. O'Hara had performed the King. The designer, who was later blown to smithereens at Tripoli, had wanted the deposed Richard ranting and roaming beneath the underground arches of a palace ' . . . I have been studying how I may compare this prison where I dwell unto the world . . .' and George, a man accustomed to sleeping eight to a room, the condensation weeping down the cellar walls, the baby coughing itself into the Infirmary, had sketched out a confined space, a simple box-like structure just roomy enough for a man to stand up in.

The local newspaper had commented in its review: 'The King's face, petulant, wilful, caught in a noose of light from the number one flood, floated in darkness- . . . when Exton entered and struck weak Richard down, such was the power of the set, the shadow of the prison bars rearing like spears against the backcloth, there was not a woman in the stalls worthy of her sex who could refrain from weeping.'

Then the war came, and George joined the Merchant Navy. Two years later his ship was torpedoed twenty-four hours out of Trinidad. He spent nine days adrift in an open boat, croaking out Christmas carols and spitting up oil.

Stella was used to such stories. Every man she had ever met told tales of escape and heroism and immersion. They had gone down in submarines, stolen through frontiers disguised as postmen, limped home across the Channel on a wing and a prayer. The commercial travellers pushed back sleeves and rolled up trouser legs to point at scars; they tapped their skulls to show where the shrapnel still lodged.

George's chief officer had collapsed in the boat. They tried to lay him flat, but he was so badly burnt he was trapped upright with his fingers stuck to the gunnel. George had scraped the skin free with his teeth. The cobweb of a hand, like a woman's lace glove, clung to the wood until the salt spray dashed it away.

'How awful,' said Stella dutifully. George was rocking over the fireguard and smiling. It was astonishing to Stella how fondly men remembered their darkest hours.

P.L. O'Hara had risen to the rank of captain in the Royal Navy. In 1944 he'd sent George a postcard of an old man tapping his way up a village street somewhere in the Cotswolds. The card was pinned to the wall beneath the moose, alongside the yellowing cutting of the review of *Richard II*.

'I wish I'd seen the play,' said Stella, kindly.

Geoffrey said it was absurd to think the designer had taken the slightest heed of any suggestion put forward by the likes of George. And furthermore, if Captain Bee's Knees O'Hara was the great actor he was cracked up to be, why hadn't he been snapped up by Hollywood instead of returning year after year to the provinces?

'Why don't you like George?' asked Stella, when they were upstairs, on the third floor, cleaning out the extra's dressing room.

'But I do,' he protested. 'He has considerable native intelligence.'

'He's not a nigger,' she said, and noticed how he winced. He was wearing a pair of woollen mittens discovered in a cupboard; he was afraid of dirt. He was washing the long mirror with a scrunched-up page of the *Evening Echo* dunked under the running tap of the basin and his mittens were sopping wet.

'You'd be better off without them,' she advised. Her own hands were black with newsprint. She couldn't quite reach the corners of the glass and was stretching on tiptoe across the dressing-table when Geoffrey put his arm round her shoulders. It wasn't an accident; he was breathing too hard. She was about to shrug him away when she thought of Meredith. Rehearsing with Geoffrey would make it easier when the time came for Meredith to claim her. Penetration, from what she had gathered from library books, was inescapably painful unless one had played a lot of tennis or ridden stallions, and she hadn't done either. Despite his Gestapo monocle, Meredith, as a man of the world, might be put off if she screamed. Hastily swallowing the liquorice George had given her earlier that morning, she swivelled round, eyes shut, and waited.

Ignoring her lips, Geoffrey nuzzled her ear. Even if it had been Meredith she didn't think she would have found it very exciting. She was reminded of the time she'd taken part in *Children's Hour* and they'd showed her how to simulate a rising storm by panting sideways into the microphone.

She began to stroke Geoffrey's harsh hair. It was a womanly gesture witnessed often enough on the screen at the cinema. She supposed it was maternal rather than sensual; it was what women did for babies, to make them feel secure and stop their heads from wobbling.

She was glad her ears were clean. Every fortnight, on bath night, Lily probed them with a kirby-grip. Uncle Vernon said it was a dangerous thing to do. Stella could be perforated. Squirming, she left off cradling Geoffrey's head and brought her hand down to separate her stomach from his. It was disgusting really, linking men with babies.

Something with the texture of an orange, peeled and sticky, bumped against her wrist. She couldn't suppress crying out her distaste, any more than she could help envying Geoffrey his lack of inhibition. On occasions, when visiting the doctor for some minor ailment, she had even felt it immodest to stick out her tongue. She didn't dare look down in case she glimpsed that object bobbing against her overall.

It's no use, she thought. I'll have to practise on someone else. It would be fearful enough to be up against something as dreadful as that belonging to a beloved, let alone attached to a person one despised. Punching Geoffrey in the chest she broke free from his arms and leapt upwards to swipe a cobweb from the ceiling. She was shaking all over and yet she felt much fonder of him now that he'd behaved so rudely. Even his hair looked different, less annoying.

'I know I give the wrong impression,' Geoffrey said, when they had finished cleaning the dressing-room. 'I know you think I'm a snob.'

'You are,' she said, 'but it's no longer an issue.' It was the truth. If he had a need to shine it was all right by her. He could spout his foreign words until the cows came home; he wasn't a stranger any more.

'I like old George,' he insisted. 'Really I do. Trouble is, he stinks.' And he went downstairs to drape his mittens in front of the coals.

Stella stayed behind, dipping her nose like a pecking hen into the front of her jumper to sniff herself. She hadn't known George smelled, or rather that the sour whiffs of

stale tobacco and unwashed clothing constituted an un-
acceptable reek. Stink had an awful sound, on a par with
putrefaction.

She raised her head and stood there, her hand cupped
over her nose to trap the scent of her skin, and all at once
she inhaled some forgotten, familiar odour of the past. It
wasn't a bad smell: something between wood smoke and
a house left empty. Her lips parted to give it a name but
the word got lost before it was uttered, and all that remained was the sweet brilliantine caught on her fingers
and her own breath smelling of the liquorice that George
had given her.

*

It was inconvenient, Stella coming home and wanting a
bath. As Uncle Vernon pointed out, it was only Wednes-
day.

'I don't care what day it is,' she said. She was so set on
it she was actually grinding her teeth.

It meant paraffin had to be fetched from Cairo Joe's
chandler's shop next door to the Greek Orthodox church,
and then the stove lugged two flights up the stairs and the
blanket nailed to the window with tacks. In the alleyway
beyond the back wall stood a row of disused stables and
a bombed house with the wallpaper hanging in shreds from
the chimney-breast, and sometimes women, no better than
they ought to be, lured men into the ruined shadows.

'You'll freeze,' Lily threatened, having run upstairs in
her coat and hat to lay out the family towel and returned,
teeth chattering, like Scott on his way to the Pole.

'You're a fool to yourself,' said Uncle Vernon. He'd put two and two together and come up with Stella's monthlies. There wasn't any other reasonable explanation, and anyone with an ounce of sense knew it was courting disaster to get into water at such a time.

Then there was the business of lighting the geyser, never easy on the best of days, let alone unscheduled. A loss of nerve, a miscalculation of timing between the release of the gas and the striking of the match could blow them all into eternity. 'Can't it wait until next week?' he implored, catching his breath on the first landing with the stove in his arms and the loofah, stiff as a smoked kipper, slotted for convenience through the braces of his trousers. 'No,' rasped Stella, 'it can't.'

When he'd fixed the 'Bath in use' notice on the door and gone stumping disapprovingly down the stairs, she pulled aside the blanket and peered into the yard. There was a high wind blowing a new moon through the clouds billowing above the chimney tops. She couldn't see any women in the alley-way, nor had she ever. They were all images in Uncle Vernon's wanton mind.

In the mirror above the wash-basin she spoke to Meredith. 'Good evening. I'm Stella Bradshaw. I don't expect you'll ever want to love me'. It was only make-believe but her mouth trembled at the suggestion. She thought she looked haunted, as though there was a demon standing at her shoulder. Perhaps it had something to do with the swooping shadows thrown by the naked light bulb swinging in the draught from the window.

There was something wrong with her hair; she had too

much forehead and her neck wasn't long enough. When she wasn't concentrating her eyebrows shot up and her mouth fell open. But then, when she willed her face to remain immobile, her mind stopped working. When she had first met Meredith she had noticed how he controlled the muscles of his cheeks, even though his eyes showed curiosity. She suspected it was education and breeding that enabled him to keep his face and his feelings separate. Bunny, who plainly came from the same sort of background as herself, hadn't mastered the trick. Under pressure, particularly when ordering the stage hands about their business, he grimaced like a gargoyle.

She wet the loofah under the tap and flattened her hair down over her eyebrows. In the corridor of the upper circle she had seen a photograph of an actress dressed as a pageboy. She had asked Bunny who she was and Bunny had said it was someone or other in the role of Joan of Arc, and that she mustn't go up there again because Rose Lipman wouldn't like to find her wandering about the passages. Up there was Miss Lipman's territory. As a girl she had been employed in the crush-bar, her arms immersed up to the elbows in beer slops. The bar had long since been done away with, but some compulsion drove Rose to climb the stairs, morning and evening, to stand vigil at the window overlooking the square. Bunny said that sometimes she let Meredith accompany her. She took a special interest in him on account of the affection she felt for his mother. Meredith had once asked her outright why she came there, and she spoke evasively of the state of the paint-work, and had he noticed the rat droppings on the bend of the stairs? He thought he saw tears in her eyes, although it was possibly only a trick of the gaslight, and he squeezed her arm in a little gesture of sympathy, and she said, looking not at him but out of the window, that she came because the past never went away, that it was always out there, waiting. Then Bunny had added, 'Mind you, we only have Meredith's version of it. And we all know how he likes to put words into other people's mouths, don't we?' It was an unguarded thing to say, and Bunny clearly regretted it because a moment later, when Geoffrey butted in with some daft remark on how extraordinary it was that a woman of Miss Lipman's humble beginnings should be aware of the theory of four-dimensional time, he had rounded on him and ticked him off for being disrespectful. Geoffrey had coloured up and marched out of the prop room as though he was putting himself under close arrest. The really extraordinary thing was that Miss Lipman should be a friend of Meredith's mother.

Uncle Vernon was dozing in his chair when Stella came downstairs. His mouth hung open and he had taken out the bottom set of his dentures; they sat in the hearth, nudging the pom-pom of his slipper, the flames flickering across them in a smile.

'I'm sorry to be a burden,' she said. 'I can't help myself. Really, I think the world of you. I've cleaned the tidemark and I've put the loofah back under the stairs.' She knew that even if he heard he wouldn't let on. Declarations, like rich food, upset him. She kissed the air above his head and scurried on icy feet through to her bedroom, off the scullery. She didn't bother to turn on the light. She flung her coat onto the bed and curled beneath the sheets, shutting her eyes to the glitter of the moon spilling across the linoleum.

Vernon waited until Stella's door closed before leaving his chair. He considered whether he should go upstairs to take down the blanket or leave it until the morning. He didn't think Stella would have remembered, not being the one to pay the bills. Come daybreak the lodgers would be burrowing in and out of the bathroom like ferrets, burning the electricity with abandon when they found the place in darkness. The poor wretch with the sewn-back eyelids would spot the difference, being in a state of perpetual light, but his sleeping habits were so irregular that by the time he surfaced from his nightmares the meter would have run up a tidy penny.

Rubbing his back, Vernon limped to the window. Above him he could see the outline of the railings and the black smudge of a wallflower thrusting through the cracks of the basement bricks. A man walked past, the steel tips to his boots striking the pavement. He was trailed by a frisky dog who stopped and cocked a dancing leg in the lamplight to let fly droplets of dazzling urine. 'Bugger off,' shouted Vernon, thumping the window with his fist.

He felt out of sorts. Stella had worked for no more than three weeks, and already she was changing. For five days she had refused to let Lily come near her with the curling tongs, and several times she had left the food uneaten on her plate. She hadn't shown insolence; she simply told them she wasn't hungry, and that she thought it was high time she chose for herself whether to crimp her hair or leave it as God made it. Lily said she had a point, on both counts.

The girl was less argumentative all round, with the exception of tonight, and that had been his fault for setting up such opposition. He had wanted her to alter, had himself at some sacrifice to his pocket jostled her onto the path towards advancement, and yet he sensed she was leaving him behind. He hadn't realised how bereft he would feel, how alarmed.

There was more to baths, he thought uneasily, than cleanliness.

4

MEREDITH MADE A TELEPHONE CALL BOTH BEfore and after breakfast in the lobby of the Commercial Hotel where he lodged. On the second occasion the wife of his landlord caught him thumping the side of the machine with his fist. 'Has button B stuck, Mr Potter?' she asked, and he murmured something unintelligible at her over his shoulder as he pushed into the revolving doors and spun out into the street.

Next door to the hotel was a garden laid out in memory of some worthy citizen of an earlier century, its beds planted with roses pruned brutally to the soil. The municipal railings had been taken away for the war effort and through the gaps in the makeshift fence of galvanised iron he saw a tramp in an army greatcoat sitting on a green bench. The tramp looked up and glared maliciously back; he was sucking on a chicken bone and the stubble of his beard glistened.

'It's all right,' said Meredith. 'I was merely admiring the garden. Such an oasis of peace in all these bricks.' And he walked on in the winter sunshine, the tom-cat smell of the tramp in his nostrils, the wind swelling his clothes, bowling him down the hill towards the station.

He began to recite an act of resignation to the Divine Will. O, Lord my God, I now at this moment, readily and willingly accept at Thy Hand whatever kind of death . . . and checked himself in time, knowing his intention was unworthy. He was neither willing nor ready to die, not until he had strangled Hilary.

He had his suede shoes brushed over with a wire brush by the boot-black outside the General Post Office and arrived at Exchange station a few minutes before ten o'clock. Entering the railway hotel he ordered a pot of coffee and sat in the main lounge with his back to the stairs. His head was full of sentences he was going to write to Hilary when he had the time to put pen to paper: I may remind you that I never asked you for a penny towards the summer gas bill . . . do you think I am made of stone? . . . surely I deserve better consideration . . . who listened for hours when you had that disagreement at Bromley over Fortescue upstaging you in *She Stoops to Conquer* . . . have you forgotten that it was I, when your mother had her second stroke, who travelled with her in the ambulance and went back on the bus to collect her plaster replica of the Sacred Heart?

He was just debating whether it was a shade pompous to refer to himself as 'I' rather than 'me' when young Harbour, the juvenile lead, tapped him on the shoulder. Harbour was extremely nervous, this being his first professional engagement, and equally determined to seize his chance. Meredith had spotted him at an end of term production of *You Never Can Tell* at drama school.

'Good morning,' said Harbour. 'Sorry to butt in.'

'I've rather a lot on my mind,' Meredith said. He didn't look at the boy but stared instead at a potted palm withering in its tub beside the grand piano on the rostrum.

Discomfited, Harbour blurted out that he thought *Dangerous Corner* a wonderful play, absolutely wonderful. And Dotty Blundell was wonderful too. How old was she exactly? He had the round blue eyes of a doll, ringed with stiff black lashes.

'On the wrong side of forty,' said Meredith. Dotty was thirty-nine, but had he added twenty years onto her age he knew it wouldn't have deterred Harbour. Not for the first time he thought how monotonous it was, this unerring selection of inappropriate objects of desire. John Harbour ought to have winged, a bee to the honey, to Babs Osborne. Dawn Allenby, a masochist if ever there was one, should have prostrated herself at the feet of Desmond Fairchild, a sadist in a trilby hat worn with the brim turned up all the way round like a vaudeville comic.

'Have I time for coffee?' asked Harbour. This morning he was wearing a rugby scarf flung boyishly about his neck.

'I think not,' said Meredith, and was gratified at the crestfallen slump to the young man's shoulders as he trailed towards the lift.

The company, until such time as the carpenters had finished building the set on stage at the theatre, had the use of a private function room on the top floor of the hotel. The room, which overlooked the booking hall or the station, was large enough for their purposes and grandly panelled in mahogany. When the trains came in or out, sending the pigeons wheeling from the vaulted roof and the steam rolling against the windows, Meredith felt he was on the poop of some ancient brig sailing a ghostly sea.

There were three men and four women in the cast of *Dangerous Corner*, all of whom, save one, were under contract for the season. The exception was Dawn Allenby, a woman in her thirties who had been engaged for this first production only and who, two days into rehearsal, had fallen heavily for Richard St Ives. If she was served before him at the morning tea-break she offered her cup to him at once, protesting that his need was greater than hers. He had only to fumble in the pocket of his sports jacket, preparatory to taking out his pipe, and she was at his elbow striking on a musical lighter which tinkled out the tune of 'Come Back to Sorrento'.

St Ives was plainly terrified of her. Cornered, he resorted to patting her on the shoulder, while across his face flitted the craven smile of a man dealing with an unpredictable pet that yet might turn on him. He laughed whenever she spoke to him and clung to Dotty Blundell for protection, whirling her away on his arm the moment rehearsals were over.

It was his own fault for having been conceited enough to be pleasant to her on the morning of the readthrough. Mistakenly thinking it would do no harm to put her at her ease—she was a plain women with the faintest smell of spirits on her breath even at ten o'clock in the morning— he had mentioned the interesting photographs hung on the stairway leading to the stalls. 'They're of past productions,' he elaborated. 'Going way back to 1911.'

'How lovely,' she enthused. 'Do show me.'

He identified several actors caught by the camera in poses of dramatic intensity and had judged from the frown between her heavy brows and the unsuitability of her responses that she would have been more enlightened had she worn spectacles.

'I was in a season of Restoration comedy at Preston,' she said, peering at a study of P.L. O'Hara with treacle ringlets playing Captain Hook in *Peter Pan*.

Bunny agreed with Meredith that there was nothing wrong with Dawn Allenby apart from her love of beauty, an affliction she was ill-equipped to fight. He put it in a nutshell when he said she was the sort of girl who, if there had been a meadow handy, would have been out there in a flash picking cowslips.

Meredith went up to the rehearsal room in a less tetchy state of mind. His brush with John Harbour had soothed him; it was always satisfying to the senses, however diminishing to the soul, to wield power. He even managed to compliment Dawn Allenby on the silk headscarf, printed all over with the heads of Scottie dogs, which she wore twisted into a turban about her dark hair.

'It is rather a find,' she agreed. 'But then I love beautiful things, don't you?' Beneath her jolly headgear her tired eyes momentarily sparkled.

Before rehearsal began Desmond Fairchild ordered the new girl, Stella, to fetch him a packet of cigarettes from the porter's desk.

'Just a moment,' called out Meredith, and pointedly asked Bunny if it was all right by him.

Bunny mumbled it was.

'It's always as well to check,' said Meredith.

They rehearsed Act One from the top. When Bunny clicked his fingers, signifying the rise of the curtain, Geoffrey, the student, was supposed to imitate the sound of a gun being fired. Given his military background, such a task should have been in the nature of coals to Newcastle, but in the event he was scrutinising his reflection in the mirror above the fireplace. Bunny banged on a table instead and the new girl gave a convincing scream.

Grace Bird, who had the smallest part in the play, that of Maud Mockridge the lady novelist, had still not memorised her lines and read from the script. Meredith wasn't bothered. Grace had appeared in supporting roles in West End productions for the last twenty years and he knew she would be word-perfect when she felt it necessary. He had only managed to persuade her to join the company because her husband had recently left her for an older woman and she needed to get away from London. Everyone liked Grace. She was in pain, but she was taking it out on a complicated Fair Isle jumper that she was knitting for some nephew in Canada.

The scene towards the close of Act One, in which Dotty Blundell as the sophisticated Frieda tells her husband Robert, played by St Ives, that Olwyn is in love with him, went particularly well:

> You wanted to know the truth, Robert, and here it is, some of it. Olwyn's been in love with you for ages. I don't know exactly how long, but I've been aware of it for the last eighteen months. Wives are always

aware of these things, you know. And not only that, I'll tell you what I've longed to tell you for some time, that I think you're a fool for not having responded to it, for not having done something about it before now. If somebody loves you like that, for God's sake, make the most of it before it's too late.

Although Dotty had all the words, Dawn Allenby's face spoke volumes; until love had struck she had been merely adequate in the role of Olwyn.

It was during the tea break that Meredith began to feel agitated again. Babs Osborne was dissatisfied with her digs. She was lodged in Faulkner Square with Florence O'Connor whose mother, Bessie Murphy, had been a famous theatrical landlady; supper on the table at eleven o'clock, a fire lit in the bedroom, a jug of hot water outside the door at eight-thirty sharp, Sundays excluded on account of Mass.

'The Cock of the North invited her to his wedding,' said Grace. 'And there was a rumour that John Galsworthy once left her five guineas under the spine of his breakfast kipper.'

Florence wasn't a patch on Bessie. She had marital troubles. The uproar in the middle of the night when Bernard Murphy rolled home fighting drunk from the seamen's club had to be heard to be credited. Babs could have borne all that if other standards had been maintained. She waved her right hand feebly in the air, as though the bone in her wrist were broken. 'Last week,' she said, 'my nail snapped off. I was struggling to set a mouse-trap.'

'Dear God,' said Grace, 'vermin are the responsibility of the landlord.'

'I don't receive any messages,' wailed Babs. 'Stanislaus telephones and they never tell me. And if I ring him we get cut off in the middle of the call.'

'Time hurries,' Meredith said, clapping his hands. He could hear the irritation in his voice. It's killing to love, he thought. And death when love stops. Everyone, save Babs Osborne, understood that her Polish lover was trying to give her the push.

Five minutes into the First Act Dotty Blundell forgot her lines and snapped her fingers for a prompt. The new girl was so lost in the action of the play that she cried out, 'It doesn't matter, go on, go on', and everyone laughed, even Meredith. In spite of this, sitting on his Empire chair beneath the window, head tilted to one side at an angle of acute concentration, he had the curious sensation that if he shifted his gaze from the little group mouthing in front of him his head might fall off. He felt for the monocle dangling against his shirt front and tumbled it between his fingers, over and over as though telling a Rosary.

St Ives was confessing to Olwyn that he and Frieda had never been happy together. Not really. 'Somehow our marriage hasn't worked. Nobody knows.' This was the moment when Dotty gave her shrug expressive of pity. For the umpteenth time the leopard-skin coat which she wore slung about her shoulders slid to the carpet. At which Bunny fussily swooped to retrieve it. 'For God's sake,' shouted Meredith, 'leave it. Stop behaving like an old Queen.'

Almost immediately he beckoned Stella and stood with

his back to the room. Outside the window sounded the thin blast of a whistle as a train prepared to leave the platform. It was as though he himself had screamed.

The girl came to him at once, her face a reflection of his own, eyes wide, her teeth biting on her lip. He told her to fetch a pencil and paper and when she brought them scribbled down several sentences in capital letters.

'Do you know where the General Post Office is?' he asked.

'Of course,' she said.

'Can you read my writing?'

'I believe I can.'

'Run all the way and don't change a word.'

Soon afterwards he announced it was lunchtime. He pretended to be engrossed in making notes until the actors had left the room. He expected Bunny to stay behind, but he was the first out of the door. Desmond Fairchild was the last to leave. 'Care to join me for a snifter, old boy?' he said, buttoning on his chamois leather glove with the hole in the thumb. Meredith ignored him.

Below the window a crocodile of children in striped caps marched across the booking hall. The flower-seller who kept a stall in the mouth of the granite arch leading to the subterranean tunnel into the street was bent over, dunking tulips in a galvanised bucket. Passing beneath the arch the children felt the slope beneath them and tumbled into a trot, the echoes of their stamping feet sending the pigeons plummeting from their perches. When the birds spewed out of the darkness the flower-seller flapped her great shawl like a matador to ward them off; they broke formation, circling the massive clock stopped at ten to ten, floundering upwards towards the whirling sky framed in the shards of glass set in the iron ribs of the shattered roof. Then Bunny, battling his way against the flow of the children, appeared in the hall and halted for a moment, the belt of his mackintosh undone, looking up at the windows of the rehearsal room. Meredith waved; he didn't think Bunny saw him.

They had met in a railway carriage in the third year of the war. Bunny was going home on a twenty-four-hour pass and Meredith returning from a week's leave in Hoylake. They had sat opposite each other in a compartment crowded with able seamen, he watching the darkening fields flying outside the window and Bunny staring down at a single sheet of notepaper, pale blue in colour, which he held on his jigging knee and from whose fold poked a sprig of crab apple in bloom. At intervals, re-crossing his cramped legs humped on the hassock of his kit-bag, his boot struck Meredith's shin and he muttered an apology, to which Meredith responded with a polite shrug of the shoulders. But then, as night fell and the lights were switched on in the carriage, illuminating the sepia photographs of Morecambe Bay at dawn and donkeys trotting Blackpool sands, he felt his privacy was being invaded and had stopped making those conciliatory gestures. Besides, from the pallor of his fat cheeks, those nails bitten to the quick, the splodge of oil on his trouser-leg and the button missing from his tunic, it was easy to distinguish to which class the man belonged. Though they both wore the uniform of a Private it was plain who was of superior rank.

He had tried to sleep but the gambling sailors made too much noise. Instead he studied the reflections in the window; the blurred beak of his own nose, that thong as if of an Indian brave imprinted across his brow by the absurd cap which he had removed at Crewe and which now lay among the cigarette butts at his feet; the jutting shoulders of the poker players who sprayed their cards like fans beneath their mouths. *Madame Butterfly,* he thought, for he had sneaked a glance at the soldier opposite and seen that he was now weeping, the letter crumpled in his fist, scrunching apple blossom.

At Wolverhampton the carriage had all but emptied, leaving only a sleeping woman cradling a badminton racket. Some miles from Nuneaton, as the train jolted with drawn blinds between an embankment, the man gave an audible sob. 'Forgive me,' he said. His voice was educated although he was wiping his nose on his sleeve. 'Bad news?' Meredith asked, and lent him a handkerchief.

The letter was from Bunny's father, telling of a bomb that had exploded in the garden. Thinking in terms of his mother's back yard in Hoylake, the washing sagging between poplar trees, Meredith had prepared himself for details of death. In his head he saw the hung sheets dotted with coal-smuts torn from their pegs and ripped into bandages as they sailed above the foxgloves. He assumed a melancholy expression and said, 'I'm so sorry. No, please keep the handkerchief.'

'There was a 300-year-old oak,' Bunny said. 'And a yew

hedge even older. It wasn't a raid. The bomber released its load because it was having difficulty reaching the coast. Another mile or so, another thirty seconds at the most and they would have dropped harmlessly in the Channel.'

'What rotten luck,' said Meredith.

'Robyn was found in the orchard with his leg blown off.'

'What can I say,' murmured Meredith. 'There aren't any adequate words.'

'My father had to shoot him.'

Meredith still hadn't forgiven him—not for the big house, the holidays touring France on bicycles, the expensive schooling, the mutilated pony or the affectionate parents. He himself had never known a father, being the issue of a man who smoked cigars and a girl plucked from the typing pool of the Cunard buildings in 1913.

Desmond Fairchild was loitering in the corridor when Meredith emerged from the rehearsal room. He demanded to know when they would have the use of the stage. Like a beggar, he went so far as to pluck at Meredith's sleeve. 'Sorry to go on about it, squire,' he said. 'I just find it impossible to get into character here.'

'So I've noticed,' said Meredith, and he pushed past him impatiently and ran down the grand staircase in search of Bunny. He found him in the station buffet slouched against the counter eating toasted tea-cakes. Beside him stood a man whose boots had burst asunder at the toes.

'No wonder you look ill,' Meredith said. 'You should eat proper food.'

'I don't have your appetite,' said Bunny. 'Nor your taste buds.'

'My God, what a stench,' cried Meredith and, snatching up Bunny's plate, took it to a table near the door.

Bunny followed. 'You don't have to be so unkind,' he complained. 'People have feelings, you know.'

'If you'd stood next to him much longer you'd be scratching by teatime.'

'I haven't got your sensitive skin either.'

'That's true enough,' said Meredith and, unable to apologise directly for his outburst at rehearsal, invited him instead to dinner that evening at the Commercial Hotel.

'I'd rather read,' said Bunny.

'Come early and leave early,' coaxed Meredith, and as though it had just occurred to him wondered aloud whether it would be a good idea to include young Harbour.

'Better not,' said Bunny, avoiding his eye. 'It's as well not to rush things.'

'I wasn't very nice to him this morning.'

'You weren't very nice to quite a few people,' said Bunny mildly.

His amiability irritated Meredith; it made him spiteful. He referred disparagingly to Bunny's demob suit. 'Own up,' he demanded. 'You sleep in it.'

'Only in the winter months,' conceded Bunny. 'I suppose this has to do with Hilary.'

'I telephoned twice this morning. I couldn't raise a dicky bird.'

'People go out, you know.'

'At eight in the morning!'

'Hilary's mother could be ill. From what you say she's very frail.'

'Could be,' sneered Meredith. 'But I bet my bottom dollar she isn't.'

'The phone could be out of order. Perhaps the bill hasn't been paid.'

'I've paid the damned bill,' shouted Meredith. 'I pay for everything,' and he lit another cigarette and exhaled furiously, glaring through the smoke at Bunny munching on the last of his tea-cakes.

The man in the worn-out boots limped towards the door carrying an ancient suitcase. Meredith, noticing Bunny fumbling in the pocket of his mackintosh, leaned across the table and seized him by the wrist. 'Don't you dare,' he hissed. 'By the state of you, it's you that needs the hand-out.'

'I was looking for my matches,' said Bunny crossly. He pursed his big mouth into such a babyish pout that Meredith found him comical; he sniggered.

'You lack consistency,' said Bunny. 'You blow with the wind.'

Meredith couldn't deny it. Often he suspected he hadn't the capacity to sustain either love or hate.

Encouraged, Bunny suggested he would be doing himself a favour if he asked Desmond Fairchild to dinner. The man might be something of a bounder, dispatching young Geoffrey every afternoon to that bookie in the Nelson Arms, not to mention the way he tapped his cigarettes on his thumbnail, but he was, after all, a favourite of Rose Lipman's. Leastways, he was a distant connection of Councillor Harris, and he had made an enormous success as Cousin Syd in that comedy series on the Light Programme, quite apart from his role in *Charley's Aunt* on Saturday Night Theatre. Appreciative letters were still arriving at the stage door from listeners to the Home Service. Meredith might not like him but he was a box office draw and bearing in mind that unfortunate incident in Windsor . . .

'Like him!' said Meredith. 'I detest him. The man's a sartorial offence. That camel-hair coat with the velvet collar . . . that vulgar hat.'

'It's possibly a mistake to make an enemy of someone on account of his trilby,' warned Bunny.

'I wouldn't stand him dinner if my life depended on it.'

'I despair,' said Bunny. He actually looked as though he did.

A young woman came in from the booking-hall trailed by a ragged child, its legs pocked with the marks of vermin. Beneath a man's jacket the woman wore a gaudy satin slip streaked at the hem with blood. Meredith clapped his hand over his nostrils.

'If I could,' said Bunny, only slightly smiling, 'I'd take you away from all this.'

*

Stella had run all the way on her errand to the Post Office; rather than let Meredith down she would have dropped in her tracks. She was quite composed copying the address onto the telegraph form, but when she came to the words: *Am in Hell. Does ten years count for nothing? You must ring. Reverse charges. Devotedly Meredith,* she experienced such a choking sensation of jealousy—she thought it must be like parachuting from an aeroplane, in that she couldn't breathe and the world dropped away—that she scrumpled up both scraps of paper and flung them into the metal basket beneath the counter.

She was half way up Stanley Street before she recovered and her heart stopped sinking in her breast. She retraced her steps just as swiftly, only to find the wastepaper basket had been emptied. Fetching another form, she wrote: *Don't bother to telephone. Will not accept reverse charges. Yours Meredith.* She gave the money for the words not used to a boy with ringworm throwing stones at a cat on a wall.

5

THE CAST WAS ALLOWED ONTO THE STAGE FIVE days before the opening night of the season. Meredith apologised for the delay. A leak had developed in a portion of the roof above the flies; there was still a slight pinking of waterdrops splattering behind the flats of the living-room set. Rose was suing the builders.

The actors, now they had the use of the theatre, grew noticeably more confident. Dawn Allenby presented Richard St Ives with an oil-painting of a bull in a tortoise-shell frame which had caught her eye at the back of a butcher's stall in St John's Market. It had been a bargain because the butcher was thinking of throwing it out in favour of a signed photograph of Field Marshal Montgomery. St Ives, while agreeing with Dotty that Freud might have something to say about the choice of subject, was rather taken with the gift. In return Dotty, on his behalf, bought Dawn Allenby a pot plant to which was wired a card saying: 'To Dawn, with great affection from Richard and Dorothy.'

The 'stopping rehearsal' of *Dangerous Corner* began at ten o'clock on Monday morning. Not until twelve o'clock, by which time no more than five minutes of the drama had been enacted, did Stella understand the meaning of the phrase. She hadn't known the lighting would play such an important part. Bunny, wearing a knitted Balaclava and carrying a clip board, called out commands to the chief electrician in a voice muffled with pain. Geoffrey said he had complained earlier of toothache. There was some trouble with the follow-spot attached to the balcony rail of the upper circle. Then a whole bank of dimmers on the switchboard unaccountably fused.

Sometimes the actors went back up to their dressing-rooms for an hour at a stretch while she and Geoffrey stood in for them, posing languidly at the fireplace or leaning back on the settee, twirling empty wine glasses. Behind them a young man with a paint-flecked beard followed the designer about the set, twitching the hem of the velvet curtains hung at the window and rearranging the ornaments on the mantelpiece. Twice, when Meredith ordered 'Two steps stage left' and Geoffrey moved to the right, Meredith came bounding down the centre aisle shouting 'Left, left, ducky' and leapt onto the apron to seize him by the shoulders and shove him into place. Stella was torn between getting it right and being manhandled by Meredith. Geoffrey was also in charge of the effects record on the Panatrope; he was better at that than moving about the stage.

The prop-room became crowded with elderly men; stage-hands and fly-men, none of whom were needed for this particular production but who were there just the same, heating cans of baked beans in a saucepan on the fire. George said that Rose Lipman, having climbed from slop-girl at Kelly's Melodrama Theatre in Paradise Street to manager of the repertory company, didn't hold with casual labour. Any day the D'Oyly Carte could disembark at Lime Street station and hire every available hand. Geoffrey said it was altruistic extravagance. 'It's not your bleeding money,' George reminded him.

Someone called Prue, who until today had remained hidden in the wardrobe-room on the first floor pedalling her sewing machine, had a chair allocated for her use in the prompt corner and a space reserved for cotton reels and safety pins on the props table in the wings. Every time the actors passed in their evening dress she was there, flicking at their shoulders with a dampened clothes brush.

'That's my wardrobe mistress,' cried St Ives, winking suggestively and hugging her until she squirmed.

'I'm nobody's mistress, you daft beggar,' she countered, beating him with mock ferocity about the head, cheeks burning with delight.

St Ives had pencilled a little red spot at the corner of each eye, to make them look bigger. Wearing grease paint, he appeared younger and yet more sinister. But then they all did, even Grace Bird. They looked both sly and exhilarated, as though they were off to some party that would end in tears.

At half past one Geoffrey confided he was worried about Dawn Allenby.

'Why?' asked Stella.

'She's got a bottle in her dressing-room and it's almost empty. And she's sitting in a peculiar way, staring at herself in the mirror.'

'That's not peculiar,' Stella said. 'You do it all the time.'

He flounced off, tugging at his hair.

Stella's main job was to sit in the prompt corner with the book. Earlier, supervised by George, she had added a tablespoon of Camp coffee to half a pint of water and poured it into the cut glass whisky decanter on the sideboard. She had polished the glasses and checked there were seven Capstans in the cigarette box set on the low table beside the settee. George said that if she put in more the whole lot would be gone before the curtain rose on Act Two. The box was a musical one and made of silver. When opened it played the chorus of 'Spread a Little Happiness', although the book stipulated it ought to be the 'Wedding March'.

Dotty wore a sleeveless dress of black velvet caught at the hip with a diamanté buckle. The flesh of her upper arm hung down when she reached for a cigarette, but it scarcely mattered. She was beyond that sort of upset. Her mouth was a red gash in her powdered face and when in Act Two she told her husband that the degenerate Martin had never loved her, never ever, even though they'd conducted an affair, real tears trickled from her tragic eyes.

At seven o'clock Stella was sent out to buy bacon sandwiches. It was dark and rain spat on the cobblestones. She ran to the café and fretted while the rashers sizzled on the stove; she couldn't wait to get back to that make-believe room blazing with light. Returning across the square she felt she was going home; not for one moment did she confuse such a place with the Aber House Hotel.

Meredith was sitting in the stalls with his feet propped up on the row in front.

'The play's awfully good, isn't it?' Stella said, handing him his sandwich.

'In your opinion,' he asked, 'what is it about?'

'Love,' she said, promptly, for she had given it some thought. 'People loving people who love somebody else.'

He explained she was mistaken. Mostly it had to do with Time. 'Think of it this way,' he urged, 'we are all mourners following a funeral procession and some of us, those of us more directly concerned with the departed, have dropped behind to tie a shoe-lace. Contact with the beloved has only been temporarily interrupted. The dead are still there, as are those we think we love, just round the corner . . . waiting to be caught up with.'

'Of course,' Stella said, 'I hadn't thought of that.'

For the life of her she couldn't fathom where funerals came into it. Besides, not everyone wore shoes with laces. Still, she was pleased he had sought her opinion.

Bunny told her to call the actors for the last act. He found it difficult to talk; having found a bottle containing tincture of iodine in the First Aid box, he held a saturated plug of cotton wool against his raging tooth.

Grace Bird was already in the corridor outside the dressing-room she shared with Dawn Allenby. 'Look here, dear,' she said, 'tell Bunny to pop up, will you?'

'What's the noise?' asked Stella, although she knew. Someone was squealing and crying at the same time, as if caught in a trap.

'Not a word,' Grace said. 'Go and fetch Bunny.'

The actors paced in the wings puffing on cigarettes, watching the sliding door in case the fireman should catch them. Desmond Fairchild got a speck of dust in his eye and Dotty, tut-tutting with concern, lent him a tissue to blow his nose.

'Any better?' she asked, and he said, giving her a peculiarly defiant look, 'My God, I suppose you think that solves everything.'

'What's wrong,' called Meredith. 'Why can't we start?' He sounded angry.

Stella tiptoed from the proscenium arch, shielding her eyes from the glare of the footlights. She couldn't see Meredith. 'There's a spot of bother,' she whispered.

'Speak up,' he shouted, and repeated, 'What's wrong?'

'I've been forbidden to divulge,' she said. Had she been alone she would have told him. It wasn't right for a man in his position to be kept in the dark.

The waiting was not prolonged. After no more than five minutes Bunny announced they could begin. It went very well. During a break in which the designer's assistant smeared the mirror above the fireplace with vaseline— Meredith had complained it reflected too much light— Dawn Allenby apologised for the drenching smell of *eau de Cologne* that pervaded her person. 'Bear with me, darlings,' she pleaded, 'I sweat like a navvy when nervous.'

Nervy or not, she was particularly convincing in her role as Olwyn, more so than she had been in previous rehearsals. When she confessed to shooting Martin no one could doubt she had it in her to pull the trigger. Martin had considered her priggish, a bit of a spinster. He had shown her some naughty drawings, to test her prudishness. 'They were horrible,' she cried, wrinkling her nose in distaste; even so, her tone was that of a woman of the world and it was evident it was Martin she found disgusting, not the drawings.

Which was why, at the very end, when Gordon tuned in on the wireless to a dance band and Robert was supposed to waltz Olwyn about the room, Stella had no patience with St Ives's reaction to Geoffrey's ten-second delay in putting on the gramophone record. Anybody with any feeling for the drama wouldn't have noticed. Richard didn't say anything; he simply stood there, every inch the martyr. Dawn Allenby seemed annoyed too, though that was possibly because she'd been cheated out of those extra moments in his arms.

When they stopped for a beer rest before running through Act Two again—a fly-man was dispatched to the Oyster Bar with a hot-water jug stamped 'Property of Sefton General Hospital'—Meredith climbed into the orchestra pit to play the piano. Geoffrey said the piece was *Sheep May Safely Graze* by Bach. Whatever it was, it was very tinkly and repetitive, and often, just as he seemed to be getting somewhere, Meredith broke off and started all over again. Stella hadn't suspected he was musical.

Uncle Vernon had paid for her to study the piano. After three weeks, during which time it became clear she might be in her dotage before she mastered the Warsaw Concerto, she'd given it up. Mr Boristan, her teacher, had a shell-shocked leg. His knee jerked up and down to the clacking of the metronome on the piano lid. Uncle Vernon had flown into a paddy on account of the seven lessons left outstanding.

She was stood in the wings refilling the whisky decanter, picturing herself seated at a concert grand on the platform of the Philharmonic Hall—Meredith was in the front row gazing up at her with adoration—when three men walking one behind the other filed through the pass-door into the auditorium. She ran to the prop room to inform George.

'They're dressed all in black,' she said. 'Like funeral directors.'

'It'll be the priests,' he said. 'Father Julian, Dr Parvin and probably Father Dooley . . . fella with carroty hair same as yours. They're from Philip Neri's.'

'That's at the end of the street opposite our house,' Stella said. 'It's Catholic.'

'What else would it be?' said George. Strictly speaking, priests weren't supposed to visit the theatre, but a blind eye had been turned to the attendance of rehearsals. Meredith had started inviting them last season. He was a convert to Rome. According to George, his sort were usually the worse; they were after redemption. Before the cast went home Dr Parvin would give a blessing.

'Mr Potter's a Catholic!' asked Stella, shaken.

'They all are,' said George. 'Apart from St Ives and that bloke Fairchild. I shouldn't think he's anything.'

Stella had been brought up to believe that Catholicism was a plague rather than a religion. Its contaminated followers were one step removed from the beasts of the field. Angels at the foot of the bed and the devil at their back, they drank like fishes and bred like rabbits. After midnight mass on Christmas Eve the street was desperate with maudlin men with bloodied noses and bruised knuckles singing 'Silent Night, Holy Night' as they urinated through the railings. Uncle Vernon had telephoned the police on more than one occasion. 'I'm the proprietor of the Aber House Hotel,' he protested. 'I can't have mayhem round my premises.' Lily said he was wasting his money, and he was; they were all papists down at the Bridewell.

In summer, when the white trash Protestants from the rookeries of the Dock Road marched in honour of King Billy, the police put up barricades to stop the Catholic men from charging the procession. The women stood on the doorsteps with their rumps to the crowd, skirts lifted to flash tattered green knickers. When Uncle Vernon was a boy a Catholic had let off a firework in the path of the brewery dray-horse and it had lumbered sideways, the streamers of orange paper fluttering from its bridle rein and drifting to the kerb. The lad on its back, dolled up as King William, had been crushed to death against the wall. The rattle of the sword he had held aloft echoed across the cobblestones.

It came as a shock to Stella, learning that educated people like Dotty Blundell and Meredith adhered to such a faith. She asked Geoffrey whether he knew the exact meaning of the word 'convert'.

'I don't know about *exact*,' he said. 'It's to alter purpose, to change from one thing to another.'

'What sort of thing?'

'In the religious sense,' he said. 'From sin to holiness.'

It wasn't much help. All the same, when the cast assembled on stage and stood with bowed heads as Dr Parvin gabbled his blessing, fingers raised to sketch that insidious sign of the cross, she found herself shivering. She had the feeling she must either give in to that showy and heady beatification or run for her life. She couldn't just stand by; it was all or nothing.

Uncle Vernon had waited up for her. He'd wanted to escort her home but she had threatened to commit arson if he came within a quarter of a mile of the theatre. He'd kept her supper warm in a pot in the oven.

'No,' she said. 'I couldn't. It was thoughtful of you, but it would choke me.'

He switched off the gas with a bad-tempered flourish, though his heart wasn't in it. If his own life had been as full he too could have dispensed with food.

'It was wonderful,' she said. 'I wish I could explain. You've no idea . . . '

He had, but he stayed silent. She looked different since Lily had stopped curling her hair. It hung straight down, neglected, lank from the rain. It wasn't altogether unbecoming.

'When I came back across the square,' she said, 'and

saw the trees swaying, I felt like Moley following Ratty through the Wild Wood, scenting his own little house on the wind.'

'What trees?' he asked. 'What wood?'

He'd seen her like this before, when she had her nose in those poetry books, and once when he'd sneaked up the stairs and caught her using the telephone. It had been one of those mornings when the early sun striking the coloured glass of the landing window had tinted the dark hall with amber light. The girl's red hair burned against the mildewed wallpaper. She'd replaced the receiver instantly and refused to tell him who she'd been speaking to, but then, as now, there was something challenging in her expression.

For a moment he saw her as someone outside of himself, another person, a stranger passing in the street with a face blazing with secrets. He felt uncomfortable; her eyes shone so.

*

The following day the dress rehearsal went so smoothly that after giving out his notes—the pause at the end of the third act, before Olwyn opened the cigarette box for the second time, was a whisker too long, and her response to Robert's line to the effect that she'd fabricated the person she loved a touch too quick—Meredith declared enough was enough. He didn't want them to become stale.

Privately he took St Ives aside and suggested he kept a friendly watch on Dawn Allenby. 'Take her out for an hour or so,' he urged. 'On her own.'

'Surely Dotty can accompany us,' said St Ives.

'Better not,' advised Meredith. 'You know what women are like.' He found himself nudging St Ives in the ribs, man to man.

Prue told Stella to collect Dotty's black frock from the dressing-room; she felt the hem on the right-hand side wasn't hanging as it should.

'She's a perfectionist,' cried Dotty. 'What a treasure,' and asked Stella to afternoon tea at George Henry Lee's across the road.

'Like this,' Stella said, looking down at her overall, and Dotty said clothes didn't matter, it was the inner person that counted. In spite of this, it was half an hour before she came downstairs dressed up to the nines in a pin-striped trouser-suit, her hair caught up in a turban of white silk.

Babs Osborne, huddled on the telephone in the door-keeper's cubicle, was attempting, yet again, to get through to Stanislaus. 'Mr Winek has to be there,' she cried, thumping the wall with her fist and dislodging a drawing-pen, sending a call sheet and a sheaf of addresses spiralling about the corridor. 'He specifically told me to call.'

'Go on ahead, dear,' said Dotty. 'Madame is having one of her turns. I shall have to see to her.'

Stella crossed the street and loitered outside the store window displaying haughty mannequins flaunting swagger coats.

In George Henry Lee's restaurant a middle-aged lady wearing purple and accompanied by a string quartet sang

'Tea for Two', circling her hands in the air as though pushing away cobwebs. When it came to the line ' . . .we won't have it known that we own a telephone', tears coursed down Babs Osborne's cheeks.

'Obsession is a terrible thing,' said Dotty. 'It devours one's life. I still haven't forgotten the misery I went through with O'Hara. I was a fool to myself; everyone warned me he was a philanderer.'

'Stanislaus isn't like that,' Babs protested.

'Of course he isn't,' soothed Dotty. She propped her elbow on the table and resting her chin on her hand gave her full attention to Stella. 'I wanted to believe he was a tragic figure,' she said. 'More sinned against than sinning, if you follow me. That way it made his rejection of me easier to bear. You do see that, don't you? He'd had a serious liaison before the war with a young girl whom he'd got pregnant. He was only a boy, hardly out of drama school and scared stiff and, by the time he'd pulled himself together and gone back to do the right thing by her, the girl had disappeared. She'd given a false name so he couldn't trace her. I thought I could help him to forget. Dear God, how wrong can one be!' Her chin slumped in the palm of her hand.

'I don't feel sorry for that girl,' said Stella. 'She shouldn't have given herself.'

'Stanislaus has a *serious* liaison with me,' cried Babs Osborne indignantly. Dotty told her to hush. 'You think you've got troubles,' she said. 'Think of poor Grace.'

'What did happen to Miss Bird's husband?' asked Stella.

She didn't want any gaps in the conversation. Babs Osborne was now weeping quite loudly and her nose was running. A string of mucus hung from her left nostril and clung to the curve of her lipsticked mouth; the waitresses kept looking across at the table.

'They made a pact,' Dotty said. 'Foolish of her perhaps, but one does these things in the grip of passion. He agreed to marry her on the understanding that he could bow out if and when something better turned up. And of course it did, albeit twelve years later—a woman older than Grace with a private income.'

'Still,' said Stella, 'she had a good innings.'

'Stanislaus loves me for myself alone,' Babs whined. 'He disapproves of inherited wealth.'

Stella thought of Meredith. 'Has Mr Potter's friend got money?' she asked.

'Hilary?' said Dotty, and laughed on her jam-filled scone. 'Not a brass farthing.'

'I expect she's pretty though,' probed Stella. 'I expect she's elegant.'

Babs Osborne stopped crying. Dotty looked thoughtfully down at the tablecloth. Stella supposed they were taken aback at her knowing details of Meredith's private life.

'Mr Potter told me to send a telegram. It was of a personal nature.'

'I can imagine,' said Babs.

'I don't mean to pry,' floundered Stella. 'It's just that Mr Potter is such an interesting man . . . I mean, he isn't run of the mill, is he? . . . and I thought any lady friend of his was bound to be unusual.'

'How very true,' murmured Dotty. Suddenly she caught sight of St Ives seated with Dawn Allenby in a corner of the restaurant. She waved to him extravagantly, blowing kisses as though she was on board an ocean liner that was carrying her away from him for ever. 'Poor Dicky,' she sighed. 'What a cross he has to bear.'

'Some people like being burdened,' said Stella. 'It gives them an interest.'

'And what does Mr Fairchild like, do you suppose?' asked Dotty. 'What is your estimation of him?'

'He's a cunt,' said Stella.

*

She was crossing the square an hour before the box office opened, sent by George to buy a bottle of milk from Brown's Café, when she saw Dawn Allenby buying a bunch of flowers from the stall near the telephone box. She waved, but Dawn didn't see her, being too engrossed in stuffing the flowers into a large carrier bag.

Rose Lipman went round the dressing-rooms before the half-hour call to wish everyone good luck. 'I expect you to do your best,' she said. 'I ask nothing less.' She was followed by Meredith who wore his monocle threaded on a silver chain. When he passed Stella in the corridor she could smell scented soap.

A telegram from Stanislaus arrived shortly before curtain up; Babs was over the moon. Prue told George that Dawn

BERYL BAINBRIDGE

Allenby was in high spirits because an admirer had sent her flowers. There was no card but Dawn said she had a fair idea who they were from.

The Lord Mayor was in the audience and the Chancellor of the University. The first three rows of the stalls were filled with people in evening dress. There were six curtain calls and Rose Lipman came on stage to be presented with a bouquet. George said she only did that on the first and last nights of the season, unless there was a particularly successful production, like the time O'Hara had brought the house down in *Richard II*.

Meredith made a speech about the civic pride the city took in its repertory company, and the importance of the drama. He said the gilded cherubs supporting the circle boxes weren't simply decorative; they were baroque symbols reinforcing the lush imagination of the theatre. But the drama on its own wasn't enough, or great performances, or symbols. They, the audience, were what mattered, for it should never be forgotten that it was their patronage and their applause which truly kept the theatre alive.

Afterwards Stella waited in the passage until she heard Meredith coming downstairs. She would have picked out his padding footsteps among an army of marching boots.

He said, 'Well done', as he went out into the street. He was joining the rest of the cast in the Oyster Bar. Stella didn't go because she was under age, and besides no one had thought to ask her.

She rang Mother instead, from the telephone box in the square. 'You'd like the play,' she told her. 'It's about nobody ever going away but always being just round the corner, waiting to be caught up with. At the very end, when the curtain comes down, they dance to that tune "My Foolish Heart".' And she sang a few bars into the mouthpiece, swaying a little, watching the lights go off in the theatre.

Mother said what she always said.

6

TWO WEEKS INTO THE NEW SEASON ROSE LIP-man, sitting in her office on the first floor, heard a cry pitched like the squeal of a snared rabbit coming from No. 1 dressing-room. It was three minutes to Overtures and Beginners. She was in the middle of writing a report for the monthly meeting of the board of governors but she laid down her pen immediately. She went along the corridor and knocked on Meredith's door. He was lying under a tartan rug on the sofa.

'That Miss Allenby,' she said. 'Seeing you're keeping her on, I hope you've mentioned the cut in salary.'

'But of course. She was grateful for what she could get.'

'And what about the new girl? How's she shaping up?'

'Very well indeed,' Meredith said. 'No complaints at all. Bunny says she's quite an asset, even if she did have a disturbed schooling.'

'What's that supposed to mean?' asked Rose, and grimaced; she was wearing new shoes and they were giving her gyp.

'She had a weak chest. She was kept at home a lot.'

'Fiddlesticks,' Rose said. 'I know the family. She hasn't had a day's illness in her life.'

'Anyway,' he said, 'she's become quite a favourite with the company.'

It was true. Dotty Blundell had grown especially fond of Stella. She was of the opinion there was more to the girl than might reasonably be expected. She had a boldness of manner, not to be confused with brashness, and an ability to express herself that was amusing, if at times disconcerting. She said as much to Bunny, who, after being furnished with certain examples of this refreshing trait, decided he ought to look into the matter.

He waylaid Stella in the paint-frame where she had been sent to boil rabbit glue on the Bunsen burner. He could hear her coughing half-way along the passage. He said, 'You understand that in my capacity as stage manager it's my job not only to train you in your chosen career but to guide you in other respects.'

'I didn't choose it,' she said. 'It was thrust upon me by Uncle Vernon.'

'Be that as it may,' he persisted, 'it's been brought to my notice that you've expressed somewhat vividly your dislike of a certain member of the Company.'

'Have I?' asked Stella. She looked puzzled.

'Apparently you referred to Mr Fairchild in these terms,' said Bunny, and dipping a brush in a tin of brown paint he scrawled the word 'cunt' on a piece of sugar paper tacked to the work top.

'Is that how you spell it?' she said.

'You can't use words like that, and certainly not in public. It's extremely vulgar. This is a theatre not a barrack room.'

'I was only repeating what George calls him,' said Stella. 'Hasn't it got something to do with horse-racing?'

Bunny repeated the conversation to Meredith, who laughed.

'Perhaps I ought to take her under my wing,' he suggested. 'Attend to her spiritual welfare.'

These days he was markedly buoyant. Hilary was telphoning him regularly, both at the theatre and the hotel. There was also a treasured, unprecedented letter, which he kept in his wallet and unfolded at least once a day, humbly asking his forgiveness.

'You don't want to overdo it,' said Bunny nervously. 'I've told her she must spend less time in the prop room.'

All the same Meredith began to pay some attention to the girl. He had already cast her as Ptolemy, the boy king, in Caesar and Cleopatra. It was an excellent little cameo, and as most of the dialogue was in the form of a rehearsed speech to the court of Alexandria it would hardly matter if, overcome by nerves, she forgot her lines. It was in the text that the eunuch Pothinus should prompt her. Suitably robed—the designer had already shown him drawings of an onion-shaped headpiece and a collar of gold—she would look more sphinx-like than most, certainly more exotic than Babs Osborne whose voice was pitched a little too high and whose features were a little too Frinton-on-Sea to suggest the perfect Cleopatra.

Stella seemed unimpressed at being given a role so early in the season. He overheard Geoffrey telling her she was lucky and her reply that luck didn't come into it. 'He wouldn't have asked me if he didn't think I could do it,' she had retorted.

He took to keeping Stella at his side during rehearsals, ostensibly to jot down notes. Her spelling was deplorable and she had a habit of adding comments of her own. *John Harbour is all right as Appolodorus,* she wrote, *but his eyelashes are a destraction,* and, *How old is Seaser exactly? Should Mr St Ives look so aincent?* He enjoyed both her company and the effect he had on her. At night in the lounge of the Commercial Hotel he and Bunny read her notes aloud to one another.

Stella had believed herself in love with him. Now, when he allowed her so much of his time, she realised that what she had felt before was but a poor shade of the real thing. The very mention of his name caused her to tremble, and in his company she had the curious sensation that her feet and her nose had enlarged out of all proportion. When he spoke to her she could scarcely hear what he said for the thudding of her lovesick heart and the chattering of her teeth. Often he told her she ought to wear warmer clothing.

Once, in the lunch hour, he invited her to accompany Bunny and himself to church. She was worried lest Uncle Vernon or Lily might see her going into Philip Neri's and was relieved when they went instead to St. Peter's in Seel Street. She copied the way Meredith bent his knee as he passed in front of the altar, and when he said November was dedicated to the souls in purgatory she lit a candle for the commercial traveller with the skin grafts.

On leaving, Meredith dipped his hand into a basin of water and traced a cross on her forehead. The touch of his fingers gave her such pleasure, that, scowling, she coughed all the way back to the theatre.

Endeavouring to be what she imagined was his ideal, she altered her demeanour several times a day. He had only to say he admired Grace Bird's fortitude and instantly her chin stiffened with resolve. He had but to comment favourably on the kittenish qualities of Babs Osborne for her to curl up as best she could on the plush seat beside him, her thumb in her mouth. Twenty-four hours later he admonished Babs for over-stressing the little-girl aspect of Cleopatra, pointing out that childishness of character was not a question of years and that she was mistaken if she supposed the difference between folly and wisdom had anything to do with either age or youth. He was not generally in favour of such a cerebral course, but in her case he felt she might gain from taking a more philosophical approach to the part. Then Stella, perceptive of his tone if not altogether sure of his argument, abandoned her thumb-sucking.

He talked to her about the play, the characters. On the surface Caesar appeared to be a supremely selfish individual, but then she had to take into account that having virtue he had no need of goodness. He was neither forgiving nor generous because the heroic figure, the truly great man, having nothing to resent could have nothing to forgive. The distinction between virtue and goodness was not understood in modern times. As for Cleopatra, she was an uneducated girl and deluded if she thought Caesar gave a pig's bonnet for her. It was Anthony whom she had enslaved, never Caesar. To Caesar all women were the same.

There was always another one around the next pyramid.

This upset Stella, though she knew she was being foolish. After all Meredith was not alluding to her, any more than he was casting himself in the role of Caesar. From now on, she thought, I shall strive to be virtuous.

Geoffrey was peeved she spent so much time in Meredith's company. It smacked of favouritism. He was playing a Nubian slave, a centurion and a sentinel in the forthcoming production, each of whom were required to utter such lines as 'The sacred white cat has been stolen' and 'Woe! Alas! Fly, fly!' It was a start, but not to be compared with Stella's debut as Ptolemy. He was even more irritated when Bunny told her she was to be interviewed by a reporter from the *Manchester Daily News*.

'Why me?' she asked, voicing Geoffrey's own thought.

'It's "the local girl makes good" angle,' explained Bunny.

The reporter would be at the stage door shortly after three o'clock. Stella must remember that she carried a heavy responsibility for the good name of the theatre. She should deal with his questions truthfully, but if he asked her anything of a personal nature she must decline to answer. The best way of coping with that sort of thing was to state firmly but courteously that she wasn't prepared to comment.

'I don't mind being personal,' she said. 'I don't think anything else is all that interesting.'

'I mean gossip,' he warned. 'Don't let him lead you into discussing other members of the company.'

'Sometimes,' observed Geoffrey darkly, 'too much publicity can have an adverse effect on both career and character.'

'Give me an example?' Stella demanded.

'T.E. Lawrence,' he replied, though not without a struggle.

'Never heard of him,' she said, and shrugged her shoulders dismissively.

The man from the newspaper wore a black trilby hat and a long black overcoat. He was bothered about his weight. 'Ignore the barrage balloon,' he joked, flattening himself exaggeratedly against the wall as the actors came out of the pass door and went up to their rooms. 'That's never Richard St Ives?' he exclaimed, watching an elderly man in a peaked cap stumbling on the stairs. 'Surely he's heavier than that?'

'It's Mr Cartwright,' said Stella. 'He's from a dramatic society on the Wirral. He plays Brittanicus. It's a big cast, you see. Twenty students from the University are coming in as extras.'

They walked to the snack-bar of the news-theatre in Clayton Square. It was Stella's suggestion; she thought the lady behind the tea-urn would be impressed when the reporter took out his pencil.

'I was a slip of a lad when the war started,' he lamented. 'Two years in the air force and I blew up.' He hoisted himself onto a high stool and wedged his stout thighs beneath the rail of the counter.

'I expect you want to ask me how I began in the theatre,' Stella said. Anxious to give credit where credit was due, she added, 'I was trained by Mrs Ackerley at Crane Hall. I got a gold medal when I was twelve.'

'It was all that Naafi food,' the reporter complained. 'Those boiled potatoes.'

'She plumped out my vowels. I tend to have flat ones. It's to do with catarrh as much as region.'

'It was all that stodge,' he persisted. 'I developed a taste for it.'

For a man who despaired of his appetite he was surprisingly offhand with the buck rarebit he had ordered; he did no more than shove it round and round his plate. Every so often he took a square-shaped flask from the inside pocket of his coat and stuck it to his lips like a trumpet. 'I need starch,' he said, gurgling.

'It's never as simple as that, it is?' said Stella. 'I expect you're unhappy.'

'I am, my dear,' he admitted. 'How very acute of you. It's my home life, you see.' And he removed his hat and discussed for some minutes the shortcomings of his wife Rita who had been in the land-army when they met. He had first caught sight of her riding in a ploughed field beyond the barbed wire perimeter of the air base. With hindsight it would have saved a lot of heartbreak if he had looked the other way. She had been perched on the seat of a tractor with the gulls flowing behind her in a slipstream.

'She looked very jaunty,' he said. 'Monarch of all she surveyed . . . Tess of the D'Urbervilles . . . that sort of thing. But I don't mind confessing that after a few honeymoon months we stalled more times than we took off . . . if you take my meaning.'

Stella didn't; she nodded just the same. 'I suppose that's why you're so fat,' she said. 'You put on bulk to withstand the pressures.'

He gave her an unhappy smile and excused himself, flopping off his stool and lumbering towards the gents. 'I'm being interviewed,' Stella told the tea-lady. 'I'm at the Playhouse. I play a boy-king, son of the flute-blower.'

'It's all right for some,' the tea-lady said. And she picked up the plate of spurned buck rarebit and emptied it into the bin under the counter.

Outside the window the day was already darkening. Across the square a gush of steam billowed from the kitchen vent of Reece's Restaurant and swallowed the sparks of a shuddering tram.

The reporter returned with two tickets for the news-theatre. He said he'd expire if he had to sit on that high stool much longer. They sat in the back row and watched a newsreel of Jack Gardiner punching Bruce Woodcock into a corner, followed by a cartoon. The reporter squirmed in his seat, and then seizing Stella's hand placed it on his lap and held it there, gripping her by the wrist. She was astonished and sat as though turned to stone, her fingers thrust through the opening of his unbuttoned trousers. On the flickering screen the wicked wolf tried his best to blow down the house of the three little pigs. The reporter covered Stella's hand with his hat.

She examined her conscience to discover if she was in

any way to blame for her companion's curious behaviour.
Every evening when she called 'Overture' and 'Beginners'
Richard St Ives dragged her through the doorway and,
putting her across his knee, whacked her on the bottom
with a rolled-up copy of *The Stage*. And only last night,
Desmond Fairchild, hearing her shouting the minutes in
the passage, had come out of the lavatory still holding
himself. Neither occurrence was as rude as what the reporter was doing, but she was pretty sure the intention
was the same. It was only a matter of degree. Did this sort
of thing happen to Babs Osborne or Miss Blundell?

She tried to pull her hand free, but it was held fast. The
protuberance under her fingers felt soft and hard at the
same time, an iron fist in a velvet glove. Attempting to
bring what Meredith would call a philosophical approach
to her predicament, she pondered on the differences in
men's and women's clothing. Trousers, she now realised,
were so designed not because their wearers had funny legs
but because men were constantly worried that an essential
part of themselves might have gone missing. They wanted
instant access, just to make sure things were in place. What
was more puzzling was why they needed everyone else to
check as well.

The reporter removed his hat and shoved a handkerchief
at her. She wondered whether she had been sniffing; it was
true she had the beginnings of a cold. Suddenly he let out
a huge sigh, as though the air was being forced out of him.
He seemed to grow smaller; certainly his thingumajig
shrank. Almost at once he fell into a doze. She was left

holding a jelly baby of shrivelled skin, her fingers glued together, webbed by a sticky emission.

Presently she slid her hand away and wiped it furtively on the upholstery of the seat beside her. Cuckoo spit, she thought, watching a working man emerging from a mining cage with an inappropriate smile on his blackened face.

The reporter woke and got abruptly to his feet, jamming his hat on his head. In the square the flower-sellers had lit the naphtha flares in the buckets set along the cobblestones. The windows of Owen Owens blazed with light. It was gone half past five.

'I have a complimentary ticket for *Dangerous Corner,*' the reporter said in a business-like way. 'Perhaps we could meet afterwards. There are one or two questions we never got round to.'

'That would be nice,' she said. She didn't think he would use the ticket, any more than he would wait for her after the performance. He was already worried lest she should tell someone what had happened. If she really wanted she could get him sent to prison. All his cockiness had deserted him; under the street lamp his face was old and frightened.

She wished him goodnight and he raised that shameful hat as she turned and walked away towards the theatre, rubbing her hand against her hip-bone like a soiled cloth against a scrubbing board.

Bunny asked how the interview had gone and she said it had gone very well. She didn't think anything of a personal nature had entered the conversation. After the first interval she took Freddie Reynalde's coffee and biscuits down to the band room under the stage. Mr Reynalde played the piano in the intermissions and could remember a time before the war when there was a proper orchestra in the pit. Things, he often told Stella, weren't the same, and neither was he. Because of his principles he hadn't served in the Forces and they'd made him do labouring jobs instead, so that now his hands weren't what they used to be either.

On the table he kept a photograph, ringed with the imprint of coffee cups, of a man sitting sideways on a motor bike. Across one corner was written in ink 'To Freddie, affectionately O'Hara'. Every time she saw the photograph Stella was reminded of someone, but she could never catch who it was. In profile the man appeared haughty, contemptuous almost. She had the feeling that if she could only get him to turn and look at her she'd recognise him. She was going out of the band room when she suddenly asked, 'If someone takes liberties with you, is it partly your own fault?'

'Liberties?' Freddie said. 'What the hell does that mean?'

She found she couldn't tell him after all. 'I keep getting put over someone's knee and smacked.'

'St Ives,' said Reynalde. 'He's harmless. If you don't like it tell him so, or else stay out of his reach.'

'It's not that I either like or dislike it,' said Stella, 'I just don't see what good it does.'

After the curtain had come down and she'd put away the props she hid in the extra's dressing-room in case the reporter had changed his mind and dared to wait for her. Her wrist hurt. When she held it up to the light she saw that a small circle of skin was inflamed. She hoped she hadn't caught an unmentionable disease from her visit to the news-theatre. Half an hour later, descending the stairs, she was startled to hear voices coming from the first floor. She had thought everyone would have gone to the Oyster Bar and that only the night-watchman would be in the building. She stopped and listened, and heard first laughter and then a voice shouting, 'For God's sake.' The next moment a door was flung violently open.

She crouched back into the shadows and saw Geoffrey run headlong down the stairs. He came and went so quickly that she might not have known it was him save for the flash of his yellow cravat under the gas-lamp. There was silence for a few seconds and then she heard Meredith's voice: 'Not to worry. He'll get over it by the morning.' She wondered if Geoffrey had complained about not getting a bigger part.

The door of Meredith's office slammed shut and he and John Harbour appeared round the bend of the passage. She was going to call out to them, but something in Meredith's face stopped her, and the next instant he had swept down the stairs with his arm about John Harbour's shoulders and was gone.

*

The dress rehearsal of Caesar and Cleopatra lasted nine hours. Cleopatra's barge wouldn't slide off the stage properly and the sphinx proved difficult to light. There was Cleopatra simpering away in her best Shirley Temple voice, 'Old gentleman, . . . don't go, old gentleman', and the spot couldn't find her. St Ives shouted, 'Can you hear me, mother?', and everyone laughed, and then Meredith pulled the hood of his duffle coat over his eyes and lay full length in the centre aisle and moaned. Everyone laughed again, but it was obviously no joking matter because Bunny flew into a rage, dancing up and down, sending the dust spiralling like fireflies above the footlights as he thundered, 'Quiet, please.' He was worn out trying to control the University students who dropped their spears on the stairs and chatted loudly to each other in the wings.

Bunny wasn't the only one to lose his temper. Desmond Fairchild and Dotty Blundell were heard arguing in the corridor, though no one could be sure what was at issue. He was supposed to have called her a cow, or something worse, and she had slapped his face, at which, according to George, he had returned the blow.

Vernon telephoned twice to know what Stella was up to. On the first occasion Bunny was tactful, assuring him she would be sent home in a taxi at any moment. In response to the second enquiry he said tersely, 'Look here, she's not working in a bank, you know', and hung up.

Stella didn't know about the telephone calls. When she wasn't required for her scene in the court room of Alexandria she was fetching and carrying and dabbing calamine lotion on the shoulders of John Harbour who, earlier in the day, had been broiled pink as a lobster by inexpertly using a sun-lamp.

A small pale woman with a pink bow in her hair sat in Grace Bird's dressing-room for most of the evening. George told Geoffrey she had been engaged to play Peter

Pan in the next production. Babs Osborne was too tall for the part, and besides the woman had played the part before, the time P.L. O'Hara had appeared as Captain Hook. Out front, yawning in the stalls, sat the priests.

On the first night Rose Lipman came backstage as usual to wish the cast good luck. Bunny complained of a fearful draught coming from the front of the house. 'There's nowt wrong,' she said. 'It's just the wind from the gents.'

Uncle Vernon and Lily were in the audience. They thought Stella was wonderful, though Lily gasped audibly when, in the middle of her speech, she had to be helped out by a man in a white toga. 'Don't act soft,' whispered Vernon. 'She's meant to hesitate.'

During the interval they bumped into Mrs Ackerley in the foyer. She was with a man in plus-fours who, she claimed, was her husband. She pronounced both Stella and the production excellent. 'I didn't recognise her at first,' Lily told her. 'She looked very haughty, didn't she?'

Mrs Ackerley introduced Vernon and Lily to no less a personage than Freddie Reynalde. He wasn't on the piano in this intermission because in the next act they were using the orchestra pit as part of the scenery. Mr Reynalde, on realising who they were, said that Stella was an interesting child.

'What's that supposed to mean?' Lily asked Vernon, when they were queuing to buy a round of drinks. She would have preferred Stella to have been labelled as 'nice' or 'well-mannered': 'interesting' was a shade ambiguous. 'Get back and be social,' hissed Vernon.

Afterwards they waited outside the stage door to take

Stella home. Other people went inside, including the Ackerleys, but Vernon knew Stella would hide in a cupboard or show them up if they were bold enough to enter. Once, the doorkeeper popped his head out and asked if they wanted to hand in autograph books. Lily said, 'No, we can get Miss Bradshaw's signature any time we want it', and Vernon shouted that they had a perfect right to loiter on a public pavement.

The leading man came out arm in arm with a girl with corkscrew curls, followed by a chap in a duffle coat, who wore a monocle and flashed a sardonic smile as though he was a member of the SS.

Stella kept them waiting a long time, and when she did appear she sprinted off down the street ahead of them. They caught up with her in Cases Street, crouching on her haunches outside the tobacconist's.

'For God's sake,' cried Lily, 'stop making an exhibition of us.' Stella compromised by walking behind them. Every time Vernon looked back she was striding with her chin tilted theatrically, her eyes fixed on the smoky heavens. 'I can't take much more of this,' he confided to Lily, and she told him to shush. 'It's not as if she's ever been any different,' she said.

Though it was late when they reached home, he felt compelled to ring Harcourt.

'You must be pleased,' Harcourt said, 'her playing Cleopatra's brother.'

'Husband,' corrected Vernon. 'Even if he is ten years old.'

'I think you'll find he's also her brother.'

'I'm not all that familiar with the play myself,' Vernon admitted. 'Naturally it's set in foreign parts. You will go and see it, I trust?'

'Wouldn't miss it for worlds,' Harcourt enthused.

'She's lost weight,' said Vernon. 'A sparrow eats more. Leastways when she's home. Consequently she's got the beginnings of a nasty boil on her arm.'

'Oh dear,' Harcourt said. 'That should be nipped in the bud.'

'It's in hand, rest assured,' said Vernon. He cleared his throat. 'There's a picture appeared in her room, the size of a postcard, of a fellow with a crown of thorns. You know the sort of thing.'

'Jesus, you mean?' said Harcourt.

'He's holding a lantern.'

'That'll be him,' Harcourt said.

'One of her lines . . . as the king . . . goes on about the Gods not suffering the unpiety of his sister to go unpunished. They're heathen gods, you understand.' He cleared his throat again.

'It's all part of the play,' soothed Harcourt. 'I shouldn't attach too much importance to it. She's at an impressionable age and she's mixing with some very odd people.'

'Odd?' said Vernon.

'Not exactly odd,' amended Harcourt. 'I just mean they're not exactly the sort of people she'd be rubbing shoulders with if she was working in a bank. And there's been a resurgence of interest in religion, you know. It's a reaction to the war. People are looking for guidance.'

'There's no call to go looking in that direction,' Vernon said.

'Go along with it,' urged Harcourt. 'Put yourself in her place.'

Vernon couldn't. There was nothing in the girl's present that remotely matched up to his past. He ordered some carbolic soap and abruptly hung up.

Lily asked him what was wrong; he had a face on him.

'I've just got off on the wrong foot with Harcourt. I meant to be open with him but when it came to it I beat about the bush. It had something to do with his tone. I often think he regards me as a fool.'

'I thought he was the cat's whiskers in your books,' Lily said. She was secretly pleased at this sudden spark of criticism leaping towards the almighty Harcourt.

'I'm worried,' fretted Vernon. 'I can't get over how different things are to the way it was when we were young. I can't keep pace. Can you imagine what it must feel like to our Stella?'

Lily remembered being cold, being hungry; how before she went to bed her mother had scorched the skirting board with the flame of a kerosene lamp to make the bugs jump out of the walls.

'No,' she said, 'I can't. I'd never even been on a train until I was past thirty and if you recall that was no joyride, simply a mercy dash to get Renée out of one of her scrapes.'

'Does it count for nothing?' Vernon said. 'Was it in vain? All that misery!'

Lily felt uncomfortable. If she hadn't known better she'd

have thought he'd been drinking. 'I'm thinking of giving them rabbit tomorrow,' she said.

'It's a different world, isn't it,' he pondered. 'She takes pocket money for granted. Likewise baths.'

'Not to mention telephones,' Lily said.

'If only we knew the sort of people she was mixing with. They may be educated but that doesn't mean they have standards. I don't want her made unhappy. I don't want her to get out of her depth. I know she'll learn in time but I want her to avoid the pitfalls.'

'I'll need carrots,' said Lily.

'I'd just like to bump into that Potter fellow she's always on about.'

'Some hopes,' Lily said. 'She'd die first.'

Vernon went upstairs with the intention of ringing Harcourt again, but the lounge door was ajar and he was seen by the soap salesman who was playing gin rummy with the traveller in miscellaneous stationery. They asked him if they were making too much noise and he said no, not at all, he was just checking that everything was in order.

He opened the front door and stood for a moment on the step looking at the glimmer of light touching the pale dome of the church and the glow of the city thrown up against the sky. In the opposite direction the street sloped downhill in darkness. Someone had chucked a brick through the gas-mantle on the corner by the Cathedral railings and it hadn't been replaced. There was fog rolling in across the river. Out in the bay sounded the distant boom of a buoy warning of danger.

7

THE READ-THROUGH OF *PETER PAN* TOOK place in the foyer beneath the back stalls. Decorated in lime-green and pink, its columns twined with formal festoons and palm trees of plaster in low relief, it smelt of coffee and cigars. Once, in the days when the building was known as Kelly's Star Music Hall, the space had served as a beer cellar.

'There are numerous books on the meaning behind this particular play,' Meredith said. 'I've read most of them and am of the opinion they do the author a disservice. I'm not qualified to judge whether the grief his mother felt on the death of his elder brother had an adverse effect on Mr Barrie's emotional development, nor do I care one way or the other. We all have our crosses to bear. Sufficient to say that I regard the play as pure make-believe. I don't want any truck with symbolic interpretations.'

Bunny was frowning; the woman, who the night before had worn a bow in her hair, stared obliquely at Meredith. Her eyes were nearer black than brown and she wore woollen knee stockings; from a distance she could have been mistaken for a child, of either sex. Her name was Mary Deare and she had played the title role twice before;

once in 1922 at the Scala Theatre, London, and again, fifteen years later, for the repertory company.

She radiated a peculiar authority—they all felt it—yet when she spoke it was in a small, flat voice hardly above a whisper. Within a moment of her arrival St Ives put on the rimless spectacles he detested, though usually he preferred to squint blindly down at the book rather than be seen in them. Desmond Fairchild was the only one who addressed her directly, and even he removed his hat for the occasion, standing deferentially in front of her, head unaccustomedly bowed as she stood, pigeon-toed in ballet slippers, sipping her coffee at the foyer bar. According to Dotty, Fairchild, while still in short trousers, had played Slightly in the Scala production of 1922.

George, who was to be in charge of the wires, having earlier walked round her as if he were the hangman measuring her for the drop, said Mary Deare would come into her own when she flew. She was built like a swallow. Secretly Stella thought Mary Deare resembled a monkey rather than a bird; it was those opaque, unblinking eyes.

The read-through finished at midday to give St Ives a rest before the evening performance of *Caesar and Cleopatra*. Stella and Geoffrey stood in for the 'lost boys'. In compliance with the licensing laws the children's rehearsal wasn't to be held until later in the afternoon. Not for another ten days would the Tiger Lily girls, recruited from Miss Thelma Broadbent's school of tap-dancing at Crane Hall, put in an appearance.

It went to Geoffrey's head that he'd been cast as Mullins, the pirate. Somebody very distinguished had played the part in the last London production. When Meredith asked him to pop out for cigarettes, he replied vulgarly, 'What did your last servant die of?' He didn't raise his voice but he intended to be heard. Meredith frowned, then smirked, and John Harbour, punching Geoffrey playfully on the shoulder, called out, 'My, my! We are hoity-toity this morning.'

Bunny told Stella that in addition to understudying Michael he wanted her to manage Tinkerbell. 'What exactly does that entail?' she asked. He explained she had to stand in the wings directing the beam of a torch at a strategically placed mirror which would send a reflection of light dancing across the back-cloth of Never-Never Land. At the same time she'd need to ring a little hand-bell. She expressed alarm at being in control of such a complicated procedure.

'It's perfectly simple,' Bunny assured her. 'Surely, you were in the Girl Guides.'

'They wouldn't have me,' she said crossly.

'It's rather like flashing signals from a convenient hill-top.'

'I've an aversion to flickering lights,' she said, 'I thought I'd told you.'

She wanted sympathy from Freddie Reynalde, but he wasn't concentrating. 'There's something in my past,' she confided, 'which makes it difficult for me to confront night lights . . . something I can't go into. Sufficient to say it's the stuff of nightmares.'

'You're a bright girl,' he said. 'You'll soon get the hang of it,' and he launched into a story concerning himself and

P.L. O'Hara on a motorcycle ride to the Brontë sisters' vicarage at Haworth. As far as she could tell it had no relevance to her own predicament. On the moors O'Hara had endeavoured to summon up Heathcliff, and a gust of wind from beyond the grave had blown the cycle off course and toppled them both into a ditch.

Geoffrey, spying Stella mooning about the prop room, imagined she was upset because she was only an understudy.

'In this precarious profession,' he informed her, 'one is lucky to have a foot in the door. It doesn't do to get too big for one's boots.'

'That's rich, coming from you,' she said witheringly. 'It's not me that goes around swearing at one's betters and pelting downstairs like a looney.' Thinking about it, she didn't mind in the least not having a proper part. If she couldn't be Peter she was quite prepared, once she'd mastered the technicalities, to hide behind a reflection.

All the same that evening in the dressing-room she shared with Babs Osborne and Dawn Allenby she apologised for being in the way.

'For heaven's sake,' cried Babs, 'you've as much right to be here as we have.'

'More, in fact,' said Dawn, who, as a lowly handmaiden to Cleopatra was conscious that, but for her age and previous experience, she would have been marooned on the top floor with the extras.

Stella hoped Babs would mention her reticence in the Oyster Bar when Meredith was present. 'She has little or no sense of her own importance,' she might say. 'What an asset in one so young.' And Meredith would perhaps reply, 'How right you are. Such modesty and lack of bombast is quite remarkable.' Then at closing time, he would climb Brownlow Hill to the Commercial Hotel, arm in arm with Bunny, thinking of her, of how special she was, pondering on her remarkable reticence.

Not that she spent more than half an hour each night in her own dressing-room. She had her backstage duties to attend to, and when she wasn't in front of the footlights she was hunched over the book in the prompt corner. Her make-up was applied, under supervision, in No. 3 dressing-room, occupied by Dotty Blundell and Grace Bird. Dotty said it was as well right from the beginning to learn how to use greasepaint properly. Babs was under too much of a strain trying to memorise her lines to be of help, and as for Dawn—well, unless the poor thing was actually wearing her glasses, the results could be decidedly hit and miss. It was an art knowing which stick to choose and where to place emphasis. Footlights could play havoc with the features. One unconsidered move and too little or too much colour could give the complexion of a rustic the appearance of a corpse and transform the face of an angel into the countenance of a harlot.

As for dressing and undressing, Stella did both in the toilet further along the corridor. She had to squat down to dodge the ancient fly-paper dangling from the lightflex, but it was better than Babs seeing her in her vest and school knickers, or anyone else for that matter; Babs insisted on keeping the dressing-room door open. 'I must have air,' she warned. 'Otherwise I shall faint.' Though the window on the stairwell was left on the latch there was always a peculiar smell in the room, a mixture of coke fumes from the hot-water pipes, peppermints and that pervasive mist of *eau de Cologne* sprayed so recklessly by Dawn Allenby.

Stella was afraid Babs might tell Dotty that she didn't wear a slip and that Dotty would rush out and buy her one, just as she had bought her a brassière after catching her in the wardrobe with her arms above her head about to be fitted for her Ptolemy costume. 'You're quite a big girl,' Dotty had said. 'It's detrimental to go without support while still in growth.'

Stella wore the brassière day and night in case Lily should see it; she would have been mortified at Stella accepting underwear from strangers.

The talk in the dressing-room was often about Mary Deare. She hadn't paid her round in the Oyster Bar the night before. At lunchtime Desmond hadn't been able to place his usual bets because she'd sent him haring back to the digs to see if an urgent letter had arrived. It hadn't, and the horse he would have put money on had won by a length, and he was twelve-and-six out of pocket. Grace Bird said it was typical, and that dressing with Dawn was moonlight and roses compared to sharing with Mary. She herself, praise be, had never been in a run with her . . . one night's charity performance of *Private Lives* at the Arts Theatre had been quite enough, thank you. 'I can't tell you, darling, how many times she sent the character juvenile out to buy cheroots. She has a positive knack of getting one to fetch and carry. She doesn't even have to ask . . . people just feel obliged to run her errands . . . as though they were atoning for something. Not me, I hasten to add. I'm too old. But she'll try it on with you Dotty, you mark my words.'

Dotty protested it would never happen, never, and couldn't help smiling. She was flattered that Grace considered her young enough to be ordered about.

Stella was seated in front of Dotty's mirror, a towel draped across her shoulders, when St Ives burst into the room without knocking. 'I shall go crazy,' he announced. He wore a hair-net and was brandishing on his fist his Caesar wig with the laurel wreath.

'Shall I go?' Stella asked, half-rising from the stool. She hated anybody seeing her hair dragged back from her forehead, even St Ives.

He restrained her by laying his hand paternally on her shoulder. 'Heavens, no, my dear. You're one of us.' Sometimes he put his pipe away while it was still smouldering and the breast pocket of his dressing-gown was burnt full of holes. 'Where the hell were you this afternoon?' he demanded, turning on Dotty.

'None of your business,' she said mildly.

'The dawn chorus was on the doorstep when I got back, clutching a bloody great bunch of half-dead daffodils.'

'At the digs?' asked Dotty, shocked.

'She said she didn't want to disturb me but she needed my advice. I had to let her in. Do you know she had the sauce to pick up my socks and start smoothing down the eiderdown.'

'A womanly attitude when all's said and done,' observed Grace charitably. She was speaking blindly into the mirror, concentrating on smudging violet shadows onto her closed and bulging eyelids.

'I had to offer her a round of toasted cheese and a cup of tea. Not her usual tipple, you'll agree. She was cracking those damn peppermints in her back teeth to disguise the fact she'd called in at the Oyster Bar on her way up.' St Ives began to pace backwards and forwards, watching himself in the mirror and pulling in his stomach. He held the wig in front of him like a withered bouquet. 'Then she told me she'd been offered a part in *Jane Eyre* at Warrington rep and did I think she ought to accept. Well, I couldn't jump on her and shout, "Take it, take it, here's the train fare", could I? Did I think it would be a wise move or should she try to persuade Meredith to keep her on for Christmas? She said she didn't mind playing a redskin at a reduced salary and wouldn't six weeks here be better than one week in Warrington? Of course, she's right about the money.' He sat down heavily in Dotty's chair.

'It's always the money,' murmured Grace. Stella thought she was probably thinking about her treacherous husband.

'It rather depends on the part, doesn't it?' said Dotty. She drew a line down the centre of Stella's nose with a stick of No. 5 and gestured she should rub it in.

'Exactly what I told her,' cried St Ives. 'She said it was the lead and I said, "What, Jane?" I mean, I was surprised, though I dare say she'd be adequate in the part . . . she's plain enough . . . and she said "No, the governess." '

'Poor soul,' Grace said briskly.

'What am I going to do if Potter tells her she can stay? You know what he's like . . . I wouldn't put it past him to say yes just to spite me. And I can't depend on Dotty keeping guard on me. Certainly not now she's otherwise engaged.'

'Quite,' said Dotty, and winked at Grace in the mirror.

'My life won't be worth living,' St Ives prophesied dejectedly. Catching Stella watching him he flashed her an extravagant smile. Under his hair-net he had the defiant air of a faded beauty.

'How did you get rid of her?' Dotty asked. 'I hope you weren't unkind.'

He reminded her that it was kindness, as she well knew, that had got him into his present pickle. 'When I said I was tired she glanced sideways at the bed and hinted she was fairly tired herself. A rest in the right surroundings, she implied, would have her tickety-boo in no time. You've no idea how awkward it was.'

'I can imagine,' said Dotty, who had served in Bomber Command during the war. 'What a tactical dilemma for you.'

'I'll have to tell Meredith he can't keep her on,' St Ives decided. 'It's either her or me.'

'Perhaps prayer might be the answer,' said Grace. 'I shall burn an extra-large candle for you on Sunday.'

'She kept fiddling with that blasted lighter,' moaned St Ives. 'Every time we got to the dying fall of *Come Back to Sorrento* she wound the damn thing up again. I tell you, I was hard put not to snatch it from her hand and throw it and her out of the window.'

Both Dotty and Grace began to laugh. Stella did too—after all, she was one of them—until a picture grew in her head of Dawn Allenby in St Ives's bed-sitter, cheeks hollowed as she sucked on her peppermints, the gas fire burning blue, those unwrapped, unwanted flowers lying on the table. She said, 'She's quite reasonable really. It's just that no one ever tells her the truth, so she feels confused. She doesn't know where she stands.'

'No, sweetie,' said Dotty, snatching up a twist of cotton wool and wiping the carmine from Stella's cheeks. 'If you must add more colour, dab it a little lower down, on a line with your ear lobes.'

Afterwards Stella was convinced she had been rebuked. She began to wonder whether St Ives's abrupt departure hadn't been occasioned by her ill-judged remark rather than by Geoffrey's calling out of the quarter hour. And had perhaps Grace Bird's goddammit of irritation been directed at her and not at the ball of beige knitting wool which had just then rolled off the shelf of the dressing-table?

Certainly Dotty was less effusive in her thanks when Stella brought her up a tray of tea in the interval. And half way through the second act, when Ptolemy accused Caesar of driving him from his palace and Caesar said, 'Go, my boy, I will not harm you; but you will be safer away, among your friends, here you are in the lion's mouth', Stella imagined St Ives spoke more severely than usual. His sky-blue eyes, ringed with black liner, were hard as coloured beads. 'It's not the lion I fear,' she cried, 'but the jackal', and although she was referring to Rufio, not Caesar, it was St Ives she confronted. Glancing at those muscular knees, ruddy beneath the hem of his pleated tunic, she made up her mind that if he ever attempted to spank her again she would scream blue murder.

He caught the drift of her thoughts, she could tell. A conqueror's laugh should have accompanied his following line of 'Brave boy', but all he could manage was a smile.

She left the theatre ten minutes after the curtain fell, running up the hill with her elbows pumping up and down, watching the clouds spreading behind the ruined tower of the church. She felt unwell.

Vernon knew something was up; the droop to her mouth, the expression in her eyes. She didn't snap his head off when he suggested she gave him a hand with the laying of the tables for the morning. Dog-tired, Lily had gone to bed a good hour before.

'How did the play go?' he asked.

'Not bad,' she said.

'Are you happy?' he prodded, wiping the damp neck of a salt-cellar on the cuff of his sleeve.

'Happy enough,' she replied.

'What about the new play, the one with the principal boy. Are you featuring?'

'I keep telling you,' Stella said, 'it's not a pantomime.' She was biting on her lip, distressed, frowning at him under her fringe of red hair.

'All right, all right,' he said, 'I stand corrected.' And he rattled a cornflake packet before setting it on the table nearest the door.

Presently she said grudgingly, 'I don't have a proper part. Mr Potter says it's as well not to rush things, not this early in my career. Better a steady flame than one that flares up

and burns itself out.' She sat down at the table reserved
for the traveller with the skin grafts and began to score
the cloth with a fork.

'Don't,' Vernon admonished. 'It makes marks.' He
longed to discuss Meredith further, his background, his
opinions—on the surface he sounded a sensible enough
sort of fellow but he didn't know how to go about it. One
ill-considered word and Stella would be up and running.

'You know Miss Allenby,' she said. 'The one in the
gauzes in the fourth act.'

'The fat one? The one who ends up with her throat cut?'

'That's Grace Bird. She's not fat really, it's just padding.
Her husband struck a mean bargain for her. I mean the
one with the long nose.'

'Oh that one,' he said, although he hadn't the faintest idea.

'Well, she's in our dressing-room and nobody likes her.
She's just tolerated. She has rows of aspirin bottles on her
dressing-table to counteract her headaches.'

'Leave them alone,' he said, for now she was fiddling
with the crochet mats of green wool, flipping them over
like pancakes. She flung the fork down, looking daggers
at him, and continued: 'The house she lived in during the
war received a direct hit, and for two days she was buried
alive nursing a glass vase belonging to her mother. When
they pulled her out the vase hadn't a crack in it, and then
the air-raid warden stumbled . . .'

'Is that boil bothering you?' Vernon interrupted, noticing the way she held her arm up against her chest as though
it was in a sling.

'I was trying to tell you something,' Stella cried out. 'Something interesting.' And she rushed from the room.

He could have kicked himself.

Two nights later Stella fainted in the prompt corner. Bunny carried her upstairs to Rose Lipman's office. Stella had changed into slacks and overall to keep her costume clean for the curtain call, but still wore a heavy gilt bracelet on her arm. Rose thought the girl hadn't been eating enough until she unclasped the bracelet and discovered the pus-stained square of lint beneath.

She packed Stella off home in a taxi, though not before interrogating her as to what she was doing with a six-inch wooden crucifix wedged down her ankle sock. She had spotted it when Stella was laid out on the sofa.

'It's just a symbol,' Stella said.

'I'm not soft,' said Rose.

'I find it comforting.'

'You're never a Catholic.'

'No,' admitted Stella, 'but I'm thinking about it.'

'While you're thinking,' Rose said, 'it might be worth considering wearing a slightly smaller cross, on a chain round your neck, like normal folk.'

*

Stella had been told to take the following morning off. It was out of the question. Lily might worm the reason out of her, and then Uncle Vernon would most likely telephone the theatre and accuse anyone who would listen of being nothing less than a slave-driver. She didn't want Rose

Lipman retaliating and telling him what had been found down her sock.

While Vernon and Lily were serving breakfast she sneaked out and hid the crucifix behind a pile of Mr Harcourt's empty cardboard boxes in the backyard. She hadn't forgotten going to the pictures with Vernon to see *The Song of Bernadette*. He'd only agreed to go because Lily told him it was a musical and had walked out the moment Bernadette started sinking to her knees in the fields. Afterwards he'd sworn he would prefer to see any child of his six foot under rather than taken for a nun.

She didn't go straight from the house to the Station Hotel. Instead she took a tram to the Pier Head and walked about until the hands of the Cunard clock stood at half past ten. She was looking forward to making a late entrance—the cast would cluster round her, expressing their admiration at her fortitude. Meredith would be particularly impressed.

It was a windy morning, and mild. She could see clear across the water to the smashed dome of the Pleasure Gardens at New Brighton. When the ferry ploughed in from Seacombe the passengers clung to the rail of the landing-stage as it bucked under the swell of the river. Centuries before, according to Uncle Vernon, the water came right up into the town, and in rough weather people had to be carried ashore. She was just imagining Meredith dressed up as a sailor and herself with her arms round his neck, clinging to him as the wind tried to tear them apart, when a man with a tray hung from his neck asked her to buy bootlaces. He had a patch over one eye and wore a row of medals sewn lopsidedly to the lapels of his ragged jacket. She said she was in the same boat as himself and kept her fist closed tight in the pocket of her overall on the one and ninepence Uncle Vernon had given her earlier.

The man swore at her before turning away, the seagulls screeching above his battered hat. She felt bad and ran after him to part with twopence, and he swore at her again. He was selling, not begging.

She was astonished after riding the lift to the top floor of the hotel to find the room deserted, save for Meredith asleep in an armchair behind the door. She walked round him, whistling, but he didn't stir. A quarter of an hour later three pirates arrived, and then Desmond Fairchild, hatless and with a bruise under one eye. 'By the look of things,' he told the pirates, 'we might as well go downstairs and order coffee.'

'Shouldn't we wake Mr Potter?' Stella asked. She couldn't bear the way he was slumped there, his bow tie askew. There was a stain on his suede shoe and another on the leg of his trousers. Worse, a sour smell hung about his duffle coat.

'Give him a few more minutes,' Desmond advised. 'We had a bit of a knees-up last night. Potter thought he was Peter Pan and flew out of the window of the Commercial Hotel. Fortunately it was from the Bar Parlour. The landlord refused to let him back in.' He took the pirates downstairs to the lounge.

Shortly afterwards Bunny came in and hit Meredith

quite sharply on the shoulder with his umbrella. He woke
stupefied, flicking his tongue over his parched lips like a
reptile.

'Go to the kitchens,' Bunny ordered Stella. 'Ask the
waiter with the dent in his forehead to give you a bucketful
of ice cubes and three or four napkins. Tell him to send
up black coffee and aspirins. And when you've done that
go home and stay there until it's time for the evening
performance.'

She protested that she couldn't go home, that she wasn't
allowed to hang around the house during the day, and
Bunny said he didn't care where the hell she went as long
as it was out of his sight.

She sulked all the way to the theatre, darting up the
corridor to the prop-room in case Rose Lipman should
spot her. There was no sign of Geoffrey. She found George
in the carpenter's shop constructing a crocodile out of
papier mâché. He was off-hand with her, even when she
recounted the gossip about Meredith being thrown out of
his lodgings.

'Desmond Fairchild's lost his hat,' she said. 'And he's
got a black eye.'

'You shouldn't be here,' George said. 'You were told
not to come in.'

She spent the rest of the day sitting on a bench in the
municipal gardens opposite the art gallery. It turned chilly
in the afternoon, and a man in a bowler hat came and sat
beside her and rubbed the side of his shoe up and down
her leg.

At five o'clock she returned to the theatre and crept up

the stairs to the dressing-room. Dawn Allenby was standing in her coat and headscarf staring at herself in the mirror. There was the remains of a quart of cider in front of the aspirin bottles on the shelf. 'What would you do?' she asked.

'I beg your pardon,' said Stella.

'If you were me? But then you can't imagine that, can you? Nobody can imagine what it's like to be me.'

'I can,' said Stella. 'None of us are all that different from one another. We all have the same feelings.'

'Feelings,' cried Dawn, and she jerked back her head and made a funny sort of noise halfway between a laugh and a howl. Stella couldn't tell whether she was acting or not—she looked dreadful, as if she was suffering from the worst sort of headache, and yet she kept watching herself in the glass, turning her face this way and that, peering forward to follow the track of a tear rolling down her cheek. 'Feelings,' she cried again. 'That filthy bastard hasn't any.' She collapsed onto a stool and laid her head down among the bits of cotton wool and the sticks of greasepaint. She wept and spoke at the same time—uttering fragments of sentences, half completed threats, pieces of swear words, repeating the name Richard over and over with the intonation of a child calling for its mother.

Stella attempted to comfort her, patting her shoulder, trying not to smile; she was embarrassed because although it was fearfully sad it was also ridiculous. It wasn't Dawn's fault. It was surely the most difficult thing in the world to appear sincere when one's heart was breaking.

Presently Dawn stopped sobbing and raised her head.

Her nose was blobbed with talcum powder; she gulped for air as if suffocating. Recovering, she said briskly, 'I've been asked to leave. I expect you've heard. Heaven knows how I'm going to tell Richard. He begged me not to take that job at Warrington. We were going dancing, you know. He'd invited me to a supper dance after the show on Christmas Eve.' She wept again, talking through her snuffles of things done behind her back, of stabbings. It would have meant nothing to that pervert to let her stay . . . he had wielded the knife, the cruel swine . . . telling her he regretted there was nothing for her when all the time he was still hiring people . . . examining her through that monocle as though he was God . . .

'Mr Potter!' said Stella, indignantly. '*He*'s not to blame. It was St Ives who wanted you to leave. He told Mr Potter it was either him or you.'

George heard the screaming and ran upstairs and slapped Dawn Allenby hard across the cheek. Then he bathed her eyes and made her a cup of tea. By the half hour, when Dotty and Babs arrived, she was sitting quietly in front of the mirror making up her face.

It was during Act Four, Scene One that she went missing. She was there to answer when Cleopatra asked her who she was laughing at, and gone by the time she was supposed to say, 'Heigho! I wish Caesar was back in Rome.' One of the university students said she had brushed past him in the corridor and gone out into the street. He was sure it was her because he had smelt the peppermints. The doorkeeper said nobody in costume had left the theatre.

As soon as Stella had finished on stage Bunny told her

to go home. For the time being she was excused from her prop-room duties and she needn't wait for the curtain call. She must take it easy for the next few days. 'I'm perfectly all right,' she grumbled. 'It was only a rotten old boil.' But he said they were Miss Lipman's orders. She was upset at missing all the excitement.

When she was dressed she went out into the square to ring Mother. She thought at first somebody had left a bundle of washing in the telephone box. The door wouldn't open, no matter how hard she shoved. She squatted down to peer through the glass and saw a headscarf printed with Scottie dogs and a hand clutching a potted plant with its leaves torn off.

8

BUNNY ESCORTED DAWN ALLENBY TO THE
station. She was going to Birmingham to stay with her sister
who had just had a baby girl. It would be a nice rest and
such a joy to hold the child. Professional women, women
of the theatre, missed out on that sort of thing, didn't they?
Still, sacrifices had to be made, though sometimes one
couldn't help wondering whether it was all worth while.

She looked rather well after her night in the hospital
and spoke complacently of the bother she had caused.
What confusion! She'd had one of her headaches, taken
three aspirins and popped out to telephone her sister. She
remembered nothing more until she woke up in the ambulance. Such an absurd misunderstanding.

Bunny didn't feel it was either the time or the place to
mention the half-dozen empty aspirin bottles strewn about
the floor of the phone box—their contents were later
found heaped like so many loose sweets in the bottom of
her handbag—or that she had 'popped out' in the middle
of the scene in Cleopatra's *boudoir*. Nor did he think it
would serve any purpose to refer to the lipstick-smeared
card, originally written by Dotty and still wired to the stem
of the mutilated plant, which, in the heat of the moment

and the fitful light of the streetlamps was mistakenly thought to have been dipped in blood.

He bought Dawn a newspaper for the journey and carried her suitcase along the platform to the compartment. She ran in front of him, head high, as though someone important was waiting for her. When they reached the carriage he swung her luggage up onto the rack and said, 'We had a little whip-round', and thrust seven one-pound-notes into her hand. It was a lie; it was his own money.

She thanked him without warmth and stuffed the notes casually into her bag. Rose had already given her two weeks' salary. 'That girl,' she said. 'Her mother left her alone in an empty house. You want to keep an eye on her. She's trouble.'

'Well,' he said, 'I must be off.' And he escaped onto the platform, praying for the whistle to blow. At the last moment, when the engine blew steam, she let down the window and handed him an envelope addressed to St Ives; she looked at him with the eyes of one waking from a dangerous dream. 'God speed,' he cried, and ran a few steps alongside the departing train to show it wasn't just a question of out of sight out of mind. She stared straight ahead as she slid away.

He opened the envelope on his way back to the theatre. The scrap of paper it contained, torn from a telephone pad, was wrapped round the musical lighter.

He read the letter not out of curiosity but to spare St Ives further embarrassment—the last thing he needed in his present introspective state was a love letter from Dawn Allenby.

St Ives blamed himself for what had happened. In the interval she had apparently asked him to have supper with her, and he'd mumbled something about wanting an early night. He couldn't recall his exact words—he suspected they were cutting—but he did remember holding his fingers against one nostril to blot out the stench of her Cologne. The memory of that gesture would never cease to haunt him. How could he have been capable of such cruelty?

Dotty had sat up all night assuring him that Dawn wasn't his responsibility. If he had accepted her invitation to supper she would have taken it for encouragement; he would simply have put off the evil day. Besides, she had only pretended to take an overdose. She was just drunk and seeking attention. Young Stella had said she was quite cheerful earlier in the evening, before she had her hysterical attack, and had talked of nothing but her sister's new baby. St Ives's name had never crossed her lips.

St Ives said it was a mercy he hadn't after all approached Meredith and asked him to give her the push. Thank God he hadn't got that on his conscience. Still, he would have done it if it hadn't slipped his mind, and surely the intention made him culpable. Dotty told him he was worrying needlessly seeing he was a Methodist, a belief which favoured an artificial rather than a natural classification of guilt.

She herself had spent a distressing and hectic ten minutes in Rose Lipman's office helping to remove Dawn's costume and button her into her street clothes. Dressed, Dawn could be passed off as a member of the audience. Dottie wasn't at all sure the poor woman shouldn't have been left in the telephone box until the ambulance arrived, rather than carried by George across the square in a fireman's lift under an old blanket, but Rose had convinced her that a scandal must be avoided at all costs.

The letter was brief and lacked punctuation—*Dear Swine, I have no money no job no friends I hope you and the girl are satisfied Hail Caesar use this in memory of me.*

Bunny dropped the lighter into a china vase in the cocktail cabinet in the prop-room and burnt the letter on the fire. Then he washed his hands.

*

Christmas was approaching and the shop windows began to fill with seasonal tableaux. In George Henry Lee's an angel with silver wings spun above three Wise Men kneeling in cotton wool snow. A sixty-foot tree, a gift from the people of Stockholm in recognition of the hospitality shown to Swedish seamen during the war, arrived at the Docks and was ceremoniously welcomed by the Lord Mayor. In the middle of the Thursday matinée a Salvation Army band began to play carols in the square and Rose sent out a donation with a request for them to move further off.

At home, Uncle Vernon ferreted out the laundry box from under the stairs and dusted off the streamers and the loops of coloured paper. He draped tinsel round the pink lampshades on the table. Lily took them off again. Most of the shades hung crookedly and were scorched on one side, and she said the tinsel constituted an added fire hazard.

'It's festive,' he argued, 'it's Christmas.' And she pointed out that not everybody wanted to be reminded of the fact. 'Some people,' she said, 'would prefer to sleep through it.' He could tell by the look on her face that she counted herself among them. He decided to take it personally and went straight out with the intention of buying a tree, just to spite her, until he remembered he could get one cheaper nearer the time.

Lily wasn't the only one who grew melancholy at the seasonal preparations. All of it, the tinsel and the trees, the hurrying shoppers with their packages wrapped in shiny paper, the children queuing to visit Santa Claus, the Star of Bethlehem on the roof of Blackler's store, below which at dusk a crowd gathered and sighed with wonder as light ran through its six points and burned against the sky, made Stella more unhappy than ever. What was the point of living, let alone Christmas, now that Meredith ignored her?

She'd noticed the change in him as soon as they began rehearsing in the theatre. She stood on the stage four mornings in a row, note-pad prominently displayed against her overall, waiting for his summons, and when it didn't come she watched the smoke from his cigarette curling above the upturned seats and felt she herself was drifting into darkness. I'm cast out, she thought. I'm one of those souls in purgatory.

He no longer bothered to talk to her when she brought him his coffee. He thanked her politely enough, but his smile was dismissive. When she passed him on the stairs his expression told her he scarcely knew she was there.

She realised he was under a strain. The stage hands grumbled at the furious pace they were expected to work. Often George came in at five o'clock in the morning to hammer away at the pirate ship in the carpenter's shop. He took a pride in his job and he didn't mind how many hours he put in as long as he got paid for them. There was the rub— Rose Lipman complained they were exceeding the estimates. He'd demanded a man in charge of each wire and Rose had baulked at the expense. He'd told her he wouldn't be responsible for safety if he couldn't have them. The slightest kink in a wire and it would snap like a violin string, plummeting the flyer to the stage.

Grace Bird reported that Rose was critical of Meredith mounting two big productions one after the other. In her opinion it was an error of judgement. Nor was she altogether satisfied with the box-office receipts for *Caesar and Cleopatra*. It was all very laudable wanting to bring culture to the masses, but if the masses chose to turn their backs on the enterprise it was the shareholders who stood to lose. At the rate things were going Meredith could swallow up the budget for the entire year before the season was a quarter way through.

Stella was forced to hold her tongue when Dotty or Babs Osborne spoke slightingly of Meredith. She let fly at Geoffrey.

'He's sensitive,' she shouted, after Geoffrey had recounted an incident in which Meredith had supposedly scuttled into the band room to avoid interviewing some out-of-work actor who had an appointment with him. 'He doesn't like disappointing people.'

'In that case,' retorted Geoffrey, 'why did he agree to see him in the first place?'

They were sitting in the Kardomah Café waiting to pick up paint and turpentine ordered by the stage designer from Haggerty's warehouse in Seel Street. The paint frame had expected a delivery earlier that morning, until Haggerty's had rung through to say the van had broken down. The order was still being unloaded.

They shared a doughnut and bickered over which half was smallest.

'Have the lot,' said Stella finally. 'I'm too miserable to eat.'

'What about?' asked Geoffrey, wolfing down both portions before she changed her mind.

'Mr Potter. I've upset him in some way. You must have noticed. He's stopped being friendly. It hurts.'

'I've no wish to sound insulting,' Geoffrey said, 'but I hardly think anything you could do would upset Meredith.' He watched her trembling lip, and added, 'You shouldn't put him on a pedestal. He's not trustworthy. Windsor Rep sacked him, you know. He was an actor then . . . in the same company as Bee's Knees O'Hara.'

'Considering your low opinion of him,' she snapped, 'I'm surprised you spend so much time with him.'

'It's only pub friendship,' he said, and flushed.

'I wish I was older,' she said. 'I wish I knew how to tackle him. I know exactly what words to use but when I'm with him I can't get them out. Nobody's ever silenced me before.' She was near to tears and relishing the feeling in a sad sort of way.

Suddenly Geoffrey said, 'I'm not sure I shall stay in the theatre. I might take my father's advice and go into business.'

'Silly ass,' she said. 'What would you want to do that for?'

'I'm out of my depth. I don't really understand them. They tell you important things, things you want to hear, and five minutes later they can't remember what they've said. I'm only here because my uncle's chairman of the board.'

'I'm only here because of Uncle Vernon,' Stella said. 'He and Rose Lipman's brother courted the same girl, only Mr Lipman won. I suppose he felt guilty.'

She thought Geoffrey looked neglected. His shirt wasn't clean and he had the beginnings of a pimple at the corner of his mouth and another about to burst above the knot of his cravat. He needed a mother.

'I'll never give up,' she said. 'I've nowhere to go except Woolworth's.'

'Don't you ever have doubts?' he asked. 'Don't you ever wonder whether it wouldn't be easier to do what's required of you?'

She wasn't sure she understood. They had marched along different paths. Uncle Vernon required something of her, but his expectations were similar to her own. 'I never doubt myself,' she said. 'Only other people.'

They returned to the warehouse and stood back as a boy carrying a sheet of glass under his arm came down the stairs. He was wearing outsize boots without laces. He tripped on the bottom step and, losing one boot, lunged forwards, cartwheeling across the pavement on that deadly crutch of glass. A man on the other side of the road raised his hat to a passing lady and distinctly said, 'Grand day for the time of the year', after which the boy fell down. He lay perfectly still, brows arched in surprise, bare toes quivering as the blood drained out of him.

Stella and Geoffrey went back to the theatre without collecting the paint. Within ten minutes of their arrival everybody knew what had happened. Babs Osborne said it was odd the way Stella was always around when tragedy struck. She didn't mean to be tactless.

Freddie Reynalde urged Stella to blot out the memory of what she had seen. She must bear in mind she was in control of the pictures in her head. It was rather like being in charge of Tinkerbell, in that she was the one flashing the torch. What she must do, he maintained, was to substitute one image for another. He knew what he was talking about, having witnessed a man die from a heart attack while forking manure. She should swop the boy on the pavement for an empty room painted white, or possibly a vase filled with lilies.

'I wish you hadn't mentioned that,' she said. 'I'm very suggestible. Now all I can see is a room filled with cow muck.'

St Ives was particularly affected by the incident. 'Dear God,' he said, 'why does life have to be so bloody awful', and he blew his nose emotionally. Dotty wasn't there to cosset him, and presently he went upstairs to the wardrobe, where Prue made him a cup of tea.

The afternoon rehearsal started late because Meredith

was at a working lunch in Rose's office. When he did arrive he strode across the stage and pushed his way through the pass door without a word.

Stella thought the play peculiar. Considering it was meant for children it was surprising how many of the characters were unpleasant, even Tinkerbell, whom she supposed was some sort of bad fairy. And though at first it was quite funny, knowing that the child Slightly was so called because when his mother had abandoned him his vest had been slightly soiled, the more she thought about it the sadder it seeemed. Babs Osborne didn't look right as Wendy; she was too big. And although it was customary for the same actor to double as Mr Darling and Captain Hook the way St Ives played them there seemed little difference between the two—he romped in the nursery and he sky-larked aboard the *Jolly Roger*. Meredith told him twice to give it a bit more blood and thunder but it wasn't in him. He was too concerned that people should like him to be really frightening.

Mary Deare as Peter was downright sinister. She was neither boy nor girl, neither old nor young. When she was on stage everyone else faded into the shadows. There was a scene between her and Wendy in the 'Home under the Ground' which caused Stella to tremble.

It was soppy enough to begin with. Babs was telling the Lost Boys a story of how mothers always waited for their children to return:

> 'See, (pointing upward) *there is the window standing open.'* So they flew to their loving parents and pen cannot

describe the happy scene over which we draw a veil. (Her triumph is spoilt by a groan from Peter and she hurries to him) '*Peter, what is it? Where is it?*' To which Mary Deare replied in a low voice, '*It isn't that kind of pain,* and then cried out with terrible conviction—*Wendy, you are wrong about mothers. I thought like you about the windows, so I stayed away for moons and moons and then I flew back, but the windows were barred, for my mother had forgotten me and another little boy was in my bed.*

Bunny noticed Stella's distress and patted her on the shoulder. 'Try not to think about it,' he urged. He imagined she was still dwelling on the accident.

She missed the rest of the rehearsal because Mary Deare kept sending her out on errands. First it was a little bit of yellow fish for her landlady's cat—the poor thing was half starved—then it was a bulb for her bedside lamp, and lastly she remembered that a friend of hers had just opened in a play in Manchester and there just might be a review in the evening paper. Would she be a sweetie and run out and buy one?

Stella browsed through the newspaper under the lamp outside the stage door. On the inside page she was astonished to see a photograph of herself dressed as Ptolemy, accompanied by a short paragraph describing her as a 'touchingly pert example of a young and ambitious actress'. She tore the photograph out and shoved the rest of the newspaper into the dustbin further along the road.

She hid the cutting in the cocktail cabinet in the prop-room—if she took it home Uncle Vernon might get his hands on it and embarrass her by reading it out to the commercial travellers. She was going to put it in the china vase, only one of the stage hands had left his lighter there for safe keeping, so she stuffed it between two books on the top shelf. She told Mary Deare the newspapers had sold out.

Mary was sitting in No. 3 dressing-room when Stella called the Overture for the evening performance of *Caesar and Cleopatra.* The little bit of fish for the landlady's cat was beginning to stink. It appeared Mary would give her eye-teeth for a cup of tea with two sugars.

'I'm not allowed in the prop-room when I'm in costume,' Stella said. 'I might get messed up.' Grace Bird winked at her.

Mary Deare was still there after the curtain had risen on Act Four, and frantic because she'd run out of matches. None of the men had any. 'Be a sweetie,' she pleaded, 'find me a match.'

Stella went bad-temperedly downstairs to borrow a box from the doorkeeper. On the bend of the lower landing she had to struggle past a Centurion lounging against the wall eating from a bag of chips. 'You shouldn't leave your spear there,' she said, 'it's obstructing the passage.' He ignored her.

The doorkeeper didn't have any matches either. She went through to the prop-room to see if there were some on the mantelpiece, but there weren't; and then she re-membered the lighter in the vase in the cabinet. On her way back up the stairs she struck it to make sure it had petrol.

*

Meredith was drinking alone in the Oyster Bar, thinking of Hilary, when a small man with sideburns and an anxious expression approached him. 'Sorry to intrude,' the man said, 'but I'm impelled to speak. My name is Bradshaw, Vernon Bradshaw.'

It meant nothing to Meredith. Still, he shook hands with the stranger as though they were old aquaintances. He was glad of the distraction, having earlier received a wire from Hilary who, at the last minute and in spite of cross-my-heart-and-hope-to-die promises, found it impossible, after all, to come down from London for the first night of *Peter Pan*. Something had cropped up, something wildly important.

'I recognised you from your photograph in front of the theatre,' the man said. 'I don't mind admitting I've been wanting to meet you for some time.'

'Excellent,' cried Meredith. 'What will you have?'

'It's civil of you. A shandy would be acceptable.'

'Come now,' Meredith protested, and ordered a whisky.

'I enjoyed the play. So did Lily . . .'

'I'm so glad,' said Meredith. He had a picture in his head of Hilary floundering in quicksand while he stood by, watching.

'We thought our Stella acquitted herself very well. But then that's natural, isn't it?'

'Good Heavens,' said Meredith, 'you must be Uncle Vernon.'

'Thing is,' Vernon said, 'she's very young, very impressionable. I'd be failing in my duty if I didn't make it my business to know who she's consorting with.'

'Quite,' said Meredith.

'I don't mind admitting that sometimes she's a little hard to understand. She's got her head screwed on, I can't deny that, but she's complicated . . . in herself. There's reasons for it, of course . . . there always are . . . but she could take the wrong step . . . out of cussedness.'

Meredith looked thoughtfully down at his glass.

'I suppose you see her differently,' said Vernon hopefully.

'No,' Meredith said. 'I'm not sure that I do.'

'Lately she seems a little low in spirits.'

'Does she?' said Meredith. He looked surprised.

'It's nothing you could put your finger on . . . nothing definite . . . little things . . . the way she looks at the photographs on the mantelpiece. She's turned one or two of them round, you know, to face the wall. And she gets up in the night and sits by the telephone in the hall in the dark. Well, it's not entirely dark . . . there's a lamp outside that shines through the fanlight. Mind you, she's done this sort of thing before. She was always one for secrets . . . we never got to meet any of her school-friends. I had to make enquiries behind her back, so to speak. I think you'll agree I was within my rights . . .'

'You were indeed,' Meredith assured him.

'Lily thought you might be able to enlighten us . . . as to why she's feeling so glum . . . she might have mentioned something . . . you being the one she spends most time with.'

'I'm afraid I can't be of much help,' Meredith said. 'There was that little upset with one of the actresses, but I don't believe they were particularly close. I suppose finding her like that could have been disturbing, but then again Stella isn't easily disturbed, is she?'

'Finding her like what?' asked Vernon, but at that moment a young man rushed in from the street. He was wearing some sort of outlandish costume and his lips were rouged.

'Come quick,' he cried, and tugging at Meredith's arm he toppled him from his stool and ran him out of the door.

*

They cancelled the rest of the performance. There was no other alternative. Desmond Fairchild flatly refused to go on in St Ives's place, with or without the book. He said he would be a laughing-stock; he hadn't the legs for it.

The girl who worked the front of house had already gone home and Rose had to take the money out of the safe and open up the box office to give the patrons their money back.

Nothing as terrible had ever happened in all her years in the theatre. Neither miscarriages nor broken hearts, feuds or fainting fits, had ever managed to extinguish the footlights. Not even the inebriated actor who, in the middle of *Strife,* taking exception to a coughing woman in the third row had leapt from the stage and wrestled her into the aisle, had succeeded in stopping the show—three cups of black coffee and a front-of-curtain apology and the play had resumed.

It was obvious they would have to abandon the run of *Caesar and Cleopatra* and close the theatre until an actor could be found to portray Hook. St Ives's leg was fractured in two places. It would be at least six weeks before he was out of plaster. They had four days in which to find a replacement. It was a catastrophe.

The recriminations were heated. Caesar had no business to be coming downstairs three minutes after the commencement of Act Four. Why hadn't he been called earlier? St Ives freely admitted his nerves were in fragments, what with Dawn Allenby's recent caper and the tragic death earlier that morning of the boy who had severed an artery on Haggerty's steps, but why had nobody reprimanded the stage-door keeper for listening to the wireless during a performance? St Ives swore he distinctly heard the strains of *Come Back to Sorrento* as he came around the bend of the stairs. Who was supposed to be responsible for the university students? Why hadn't somebody checked that they hadn't left their spears for all and sundry to trip over?

Bunny was so choked at what he termed veiled inferences and an unfair proportioning of blame that he stalked out of Rose's office. He fled to the prop-room, where he found John Harbour and Babs, huddled whispering round the fire with Freddie Reynalde. Dotty and Grace had gone in the ambulance with St Ives and Desmond Fairchild was in the Oyster Bar making the most of the unexpected drinking time.

Harbour had been in the middle of telling Freddie that in his opinion it was *almost* a blessing that the theatre would have to close. It was ghastly for poor Richard, breaking his leg and all that, but at least it meant there would be an extension of rehearsals for *Peter Pan.* The production was a shambles at the moment. Babs said it was all very well but had he forgotten their leading man was flat on his back in Sefton General?

They stopped talking when Bunny came in, shocked into silence at the expression on his face. He was pressing his fists against his stomach as though he had suffered an internal injury. 'I've given the best years of my life,' he faltered, and was unable to say more. He turned away from them and struggled for control. Discomfited, they stared at his heaving shoulders.

He was tracked down almost immediately by Meredith, sent by Rose to fetch him back.

'I'm not coming,' he replied, his voice wobbling with emotion. 'I'm thinking of handing in my resignation.'

'Don't talk rot,' said Meredith and, taking him by the arm, frog-marched him along the corridor.

Five minutes later John Harbour was dispatched to the Oyster Bar to tell Desmond Fairchild he was wanted in Rose's office.

Desmond took his time, and when he finally arrived and the proposition was put to him, he shook his head. He had no ambitions to play Hook and certainly not at four days' notice. He hadn't been offered the part in the first place and was more than content in the role of Smee.

He stood there in his camel-hair coat, tapping a cigarette on his thumbnail. 'Sorry, Squire,' he said, 'but I know my limitations.' He smiled spitefully.

Meredith telephoned several numbers without success. George Rudd was on tour; Michael Lamonte, according to his lady friend, was filming at Pinewood; Berenson had left the business for school-teaching and wasn't about to throw it up, thank you, for all the tea in China, and did Meredith realise it was gone midnight?

An actor who had written to Meredith on many occasions—always enclosing, as his wife was at pains to point out, his page number in *Spotlight* and a stamped addressed envelope, without ever once receiving so much as an acknowledgement in return—was unfortunately dead. Bunny remembered Cyril Someone-or-other, who had been fearfully good in a revival of 'Sheppy' at Watford before the war. Meredith reminded him that Cyril thingumajig had lost both legs in a skirmish in North Africa.

It was then that Rose, distractedly rearranging the framed photographs on her desk top, thought of O'Hara.

'No,' shouted Meredith. Bringing his voice under control he suggested it was unlikely that a man of O'Hara's established reputation would want to appear in the provinces.

'Fiddlesticks,' said Rose, 'if he's not working he'll jump at it, for old time's sake.' She couldn't think why it hadn't occurred to her sooner.

Bunny stood at the window and stared wearily down into the lamp-lit street. A figure in a raincoat was preparing for sleep in the doorway of George Henry Lee's, treading round and round on a heap of old newspapers like a dog at the hearth.

Bunny felt in his pocket, fiddling for loose change.

9

O'HARA'S LANDLADY CALLED UP THE STAIRS that he was wanted on the telephone. 'Long distance,' she said.

When he heard Potter's voice he was taken aback. 'How are you?' he asked, and was annoyed with himself for sounding so effusive.

'I must apologise for disturbing you at such a late hour,' Potter said. There was that familiar intake of breath as he drew on a cigarette. 'Rose felt we couldn't leave it until the morning. Reynalde gave me your number.'

He explained, briefly, the difficulties they were in. 'I don't expect you'll want to come up here . . . even if you're available.'

O'Hara reminded him that Jung had considered Liverpool the centre of the Universe.

'How interesting,' said Potter. 'I take it he didn't live here. It'll be a six-week run, two matinées a week, from Tuesday.'

'I presume I'll be doubling up on both parts,' O'Hara said.

'But of course. It's traditional.'

'Not invariably,' said O'Hara. 'Laughton only played Hook.'

Aferwards he telephoned Lizzie to ask what she thought.

'Christmas in the provinces,' she said. 'It's not everybody's cup of tea, is it? Still, you've always wanted to go back, and I dare say you can demand the earth in salary.'

'But think about it . . . Potter of all people.'

'I am thinking,' she said. 'It was donkey's years ago.'

'We can never measure the effect we have on other people,' he said, although he, more than most, had a fair idea. 'Time has nothing to do with it.'

'Who else will be up there,' she enquired, 'besides Mary Deare?'

'Dotty probably. I didn't ask.'

'And when are you off?'

'As soon as I've packed. I shall ride up on the Norton,' he told her, and there was a difficult pause in which she waited for him to sugest she should come up to Liverpool in the New Year.

'Well then,' she said, at last. 'Don't forget to send a postcard.'

Frowning, he rang Mona Gage and hung up when her husband answered.

*

Rose booked O'Hara into the Adelphi Hotel at the theatre's expense. It was an empty gesture—she knew he wouldn't stay there. He had always, even as a young man, hankered for the past.

After only one night he went out and rented his old

room in the front basement of a house in Percy Street. He sought, self-consciously, now that he once again walked those familiar streets, to catch up with that other, vanished self who, at this distance, seemed more real than the person he had become.

The room hadn't changed. The fire still smoked, the damp still grew vegetable growths the colour of peaches on the wall between the grimy windows. Even the table that Keeley, the painter, had used as a palette was in its place beneath the sink. He didn't dare inspect the mattress in case that too was the same.

When he dragged out the table and the lamplight spilled onto the splodges of cadmium yellow and scarlet lake, he thought of the girl who had shown him to his dressing-room on the morning of his arrival. She was dressed as a munitions worker, and when he switched on the light her hair had blazed under the dim bulb. 'I know this is your old dressing-room,' she said. 'George told me.'

'Ah, George,' he repeated. 'Salt of the earth.'

'You still have to kick the pipes before the water comes out of the tap,' she said.

Outside, the gate had gone from the basement steps, and the slanting roof of the coal hole had fallen in, but when he looked he could see the chafed paint, those marks on the rusted railings, where once he had padlocked his motorcycle.

Keeley, of course, had long since departed. A biology student with a stutter now occupied the back room. He was lonely and broke and had already barged in for the loan of a cupful of Quaker oats.

Those first evenings O'Hara avoided going to the Oyster Bar. Grace Bird, whom he had worked with before and of whom he was fond, spent most nights up at the hospital knitting in the waiting-room while Dotty ministered to poor old Dickie St Ives, and although he respected Mary Deare as a performer—she was possibly the best Peter since Nina Boucicault—she had never been a chum. He rather took to Bunny, but it was obvious the stage-manager was a crony of Potter's and it was advisable, this early on, to leave well alone. To be fair, Potter was behaving better than would have been expected—cold yet civil.

It was no hardship isolating himself. He had no wish for company nor wanted to be anywhere else than in that room with the paint-flecked table. He lay on the narrow bed and waited for the basement gate to bang in the windswept night, until he remembered it was no longer there.

Dotty had once gone out with a piece of string to stop its clanging. Dotty had pinned a photograph of Charles Laughton, torn from a movie magazine, on the wall above the fireplace. If he got up and peered closely enough he would still see the prick of that vanished drawing-pin in the plaster.

The girl behind the beauty-counter at Lewis's had scrawled her name in pencil on the window frame. Then you won't forget me, she had said. But he had, long before the condensation, dribbling, like Dotty's tears, had smeared the name away.

Dotty had cried a lot. He had only to go for a spin with Freddie Reynalde or spend half an hour too long in the pub for her shoulders to slump and her eyes to fill. Once, she'd taken a hammer to the headlamp of his motorcycle. She'd done it because she cared. It was no good repressing her feelings. It struck him as convenient the way women placed such reliance on their emotions.

She'd offered to lend him the money to have the bike fixed, and when he accepted she said, 'I've broken something precious, haven't I?' and knelt in the street among the bits of glass, looking up at him as if she understood it was more than a lamp she had smashed.

He forgave her, and then a week later he and Keeley came home from the Beaux Arts Club to find her sitting on the basement steps, smiling nice as pie. Fooled, he let her in, and she ran straight to his jazz records and whipping off her court shoe brought the heel down on his favourite Blossom Dearie.

This time it was because her feelings told her he didn't love her. She dragged up that other business he'd been foolish enough to confide in her, that lost girl with the golden voice. No wonder *she*'d disappeared into the wide blue yonder. He was a monster. Why, in all the time she'd known him he had never said the *words*.

'What words?' he asked, and she said, 'Exactly. You don't begin to know what I mean.' And then Keeley had nudged him and he'd found the words she wanted, and still it wasn't enough—she called him a liar and wept even louder.

He'd thought he did love her, until she went on worrying at it, thrashing it to and fro, churning up feelings like a dog digging up a bone. By the time she was through he didn't know what he felt.

He'd had no such doubts when embracing that model

Keeley had brought home from the Art School. She had tufts of hair in her armpits like clumps of grass. A man couldn't slide into the abyss when she was around.

He'd told Dotty she wouldn't always feel so unhappy, that one day she'd look at him and his face would seem quite ordinary, and she'd flown at him, pummeling his chest with her fists, sobbing that the day would never come.

They were both young, of course, and neither of them knew what they were talking about. Keeley said girls were unreasonable because they weren't any good at sport— they hadn't learnt any rules.

At his first rehearsal of *Peter Pan,* almost before Bunny had finished introducing him to the rest of the cast, Dotty had taken him proprietorially by the arm and strolled him into the wings. There was no need for her to be present. She was playing Mrs Darling and she and Hook were never on stage together.

He thought, how changed she is, how nearly old she has become. She wore a smart blue costume with a tiny hat tilted over one eye. She whispered, 'How strange it is, you and I here together . . . after all these years.' Then he thought, how little she has altered. She chided him for not responding to her Christmas cards. 'One every year,' she cried reproachfully. 'Without fail. But then, you were never one to dwell on the past, were you?'

In spite of this, she never lost an opportunity to jog his memory, mostly during the coffee breaks when Desmond Fairchild and the girl with red hair were within earshot.

'Remember that time we went dancing at the Rialto

ballroom,' she would say. 'After the second night of *Richard II* . . . when that fight broke out? There were bottles of stout flying like skittles.' Or, 'Wasn't it a scream that afternoon we went to the matinée at the Court and you got a fit of the hiccoughs.' And Mou-Mou! . . . How fond he had been of darling Mou-Mou . . . it broke Mummy's heart to have her put down, but it was the kindest thing to do. . . 'You must have got my letter,' she said. 'It was some years back.'

'No,' he said. 'I'm afraid I didn't. It must have been after I moved.'

'But, of course,' she said. 'Otherwise you would have replied.'

He didn't mind. There was nothing so cosily malicious, once it was mutually accepted, as dead love, and besides it was plain Dotty had a thing going with Fairchild. The man had a faint discoloration under one eye—he couldn't help speculating whether Dotty hadn't been giving him a hard time.

He discovered the girl's name was Stella and tried to engage her in gossip. She eyed him shrewdly and said Mr Fairchild was very nice, very nice indeed, and so was Miss Blundell. Miss Blundell had been particularly nice to her. 'It's nice when people are nice, isn't it?' he said, and she snapped back, 'I do know other words, but usually nobody likes the sound of them.' She reminded him of someone, or rather he felt he had met her before.

'It's hardly likely,' Freddie Reynalde pointed out. 'You haven't been in this neck of the woods for years, and I doubt if in all her life she's been further than Blackpool.'

*

The first dress-rehearsal lasted the whole of Saturday. Bunny had taken the precaution of holding separate flying- and lighting-rehearsals on the Friday, with the result that the delays were structural rather than technical—the deck of the *Jolly Roger* swayed alarmingly during the fight between the pirates and the Lost Boys, and the ticking of the crocodile was found to be inaudible beyond the first three rows of the stalls. When Hook, communing with his ego, murmured, *'How still the night is; nothing sounds alive . . . split my infinitives, but 'tis my hour of triumph'*, the mast creaked ominously and all but fell against the backcloth.

In spite of this, those actors who stole into the auditorium between entrances returned full of enthusiasm. John Harbour pronounced the production nothing short of magical. The missed cues, the botching of business, the somewhat lumpy prancings of the Tiger Lily troupe counted for nothing beside the chilling authority of Hook and the strutting Peter, unearthly yet real of Mary Deare. O'Hara, he said, was the terrifying shadow on the wall which every child saw through half-closed lids once the nursery door had shut. Not many of those present had first-hand knowledge of such rarified accommodation, but they took his meaning.

In Act Five, Father Dooley, who had been sipping Irish whisky from a camouflaged army-issue water-bottle, responded dramatically to the exchange between Hook and Wendy.

(Wendy is brought up from the hold and sees at a glance that the deck hasn't been scrubbed for years.)

Hook:	So my beauty, you are to see your children walk the plank.
Wendy:	(with noble calmness): Are they to die?
Hook:	They are. Silence all, for a mother's last words to her children.
Wendy:	These are my last words. Dear boys, I feel that I have a message for you from your real mothers, and it is this: we hope our sons will die like Englishmen.

At which Father Dooley rose unsteadily in his seat and denounced the philosophy behind the words. Nobody on stage heard him. Grace, who was purling in the front circle, gathered he was drawing their attention to the war and the number of dead and maimed. Meredith endeavoured to explain that the play had been written long before the carnage of the First World War, let alone the Second. Besides in 1915 Mr Barrie had written to George, his adopted son and one of the original Lost Boys, that he no longer thought of war as glorious. *It is just unspeakably monstrous to me now.* To clinch matters, a few days later George was killed, shot through the head as his battalion advanced on St Eloi.

Father Dooley refused to see the connection and continued to protest. Dr Parvin took him home. Meredith, who had served in nothing more bloody than the Catering Corps, called a break and clambered into the orchestra pit to mangle Bach on the piano.

*

After the national anthem, and before the curtain went up, Rose made a speech expressing her mixed emotions at the unfortunate accident which had befallen Richard St Ives. Mixed, she said, because it had given the theatre the opportunity to invite P.L. O'Hara to step into the breach. She drew the audience's attention to the injured leading man, who, leg propped on a cushioned trestle arrangement protruding into the centre aisle, sat under a red blanket in the third row of the stalls. He was given an ovation, and Rushworth's grand-daughter, a stout girl with ringlets, ran forward and, leaning heavily against his broken leg, presented him with a bouquet. It was this same child who later screamed piercingly when Hook made his first entrance, clawing the misty air above the frozen river.

After the final curtain-call Bunny came into the prop-room and invited Stella to a little party at the Commercial Hotel. The play had overrun the licensing hours and the Oyster Bar was already closed. 'It might amuse you,' he said, and added gallanty, 'You aquitted yourself excellently with the torch.'

'Thank you very much,' she said. She longed to go, and yet she couldn't bear the idea.

'You too, George,' said Bunny.

George wriggled out of it. His missus would go on a vinegar trip if he was late home again.

Stella ran upstairs and combed her hair in the extras' dressing-room. She thought of taking off her overall—she was wearing one of Lily's blouses underneath—only when it was unbuttoned and she looked in the mirror her chest poked out in a most peculiar way. She imagined it might settle down if she removed her brassière, but what if Dotty noticed and made some personal remark about her growth?

She couldn't think how she was going to enter the Commercial Hotel, not unless accompanied or pushed. No doubt Babs and Grace would travel up the hill by taxi. Trouble was, if she appeared downstairs too soon it would look as if she was cadging a lift, and if she arrived too late they would have gone without her—and than how would she summon up the courage to go at all?

She went to find Geoffrey. The stage doorkeeper said he had already left. At last, emerging into the street, she found herself a hundred yards behind John Harbour and Meredith. Squatting, she pretended to tie a non-existent shoe-lace and waited until the two men had crossed Clayton Square and turned the corner in the direction of Bold Street.

I can't go, she thought. Who needs parties? And she began to walk home the long way round so as not to bump into anybody. She felt annoyed with herself, made miserable with so little cause. If she had been the offspring of drunken parents in Scotland Road, or born with a hairlip like Ma Tang's daughter, there might be some excuse for feeling as she did. Why couldn't she slide out of herself and be someone else, if only for the ten seconds it would take to push open the door of the hotel and step across the threshold?

She was making for the telephone box outside the Broken Dolls Hospital when she heard the puttering of a motocycle engine as it reduced speed in the gutter behind her. Turning, she recognised O'Hara. He wore the flying helmet he had affected on the morning of his arrival and those goggles which, when removed, had left him looking like a barn owl, white-ringed eyes blinking in a smut-flecked face.

'Hop on,' he said, patting the pillion.

She clung to the waist of his crackling leather overcoat as they thundered up the hill and roared along Hope Street, past the Mission Hall and the Institute and the ruined silhouette of the Methodist church. The headlamp picked out a cat streaking towards a wall, and a child without shoes between the shafts of a wooden cart, straining to pull it into an alleyway, and both images were gone in an instant, drowned in darkness as the bike sped past, the road a triangle of bright water as they rode the glittering breakers of the tramlines and swerved to the kerb of the Commercial Hotel.

Meredith's landlord had put the back parlour at their disposal. There was a fire in the hearth and sandwiches on the sideboard. One of the pirates gave Stella a glass half-full of gin. She swallowed it in one gulp and started to cough.

Toasts were drunk to Mary Deare and O'Hara. It had been a wonderful night, absolutely marvellous. It couldn't have gone better. Seven curtain calls, and they would have taken more if Rose, concerned at the overtime the stage-hands were in danger of earning, hadn't signalled Freddie Reynalde to play the audience out.

What about that child who had screamed in Act Two, and the hissing that had followed . . . and the outbreak of sobbing when Tinkerbell drank the poison and Peter announced she was dying . . . and the sigh that had rippled . . . yes, rippled through the theatre when Peter, alone on the rock in the lagoon, heard the mermaid's melancholy cry as the moon began to rise over Never-Never Land.

O'Hara, on behalf of the company, spoke a few words in appreciation of Meredith. He said he'd done a wonderful job in very difficult circumstances. The lighting had been quite brilliant.

Meredith, wearing his duffle-coat and sitting cross-legged on the floor, raised his glass in response. 'How very kind,' he murmured. 'Such praise, coming from you.'

Stella asked John Harbour if he had seen Geoffrey.

'He's off sulking most likely,' said Harbour, and started to tell her his reasons for believing O'Hara's performance that evening had been the equal of any of the great Shakespearian roles as portrayed by the likes of Ralphie or Larry. 'He had the audience in the palm of his hand,' he cried. 'How they hated him. Those flourishes, those poses, that diabolical smile . . . the appalling courtesy of his gestures . . .' He broke off in mid-sentence, as if suddenly realising who he was talking to, and abruptly left her for Mary Deare. Sitting at her feet he gazed up into her withered child's face and began again. 'You had the audience in the palm of your hand. How they loved you.'

O'Hara had been buttonholed by Babs Osborne. She was reading him parts of a letter from some fellow with a foreign name. 'Listen to this bit,' she urged. ' *"I do not wish to treat you like a good-time girl. Were my feelings not so strong I could not bring myself to say goodbye."* You can tell the torment he's in, can't you? It's obvious isn't it, that he still loves me?'

'Yes,' said O'Hara. 'It couldn't be more obvious.' He was watching Stella who stood at the fireplace, leaning against the armchair in which Potter now sat holding court. She had black eyebrows despite the colour of her hair, and a little Roman nose.

'Why can't he treat me like a good-time girl,' wailed Babs. 'It's better than nothing, isn't it?'

Stella was feeling decidedly confident. I've cut the ropes that bind me to the shore, she thought, and sinking down onto the arm of Meredith's chair she listened, smiling, to one of the pirates confiding that when he was in town he consulted the same dentist as dear Johnny. He'd once had a drink with him in the Shaftesbury—Johnny, not the dentist—and really, he couldn't have been sweeter. There was no side to him, absolutely none. Of course, there had been lots of other people present. He couldn't pretend there'd been just the two of them.'

'Quite,' said Meredith, and yawned.

Someone put a dance record on the gramophone and presently Desmond Fairchild and Dotty swayed together in a corner of the room. She had bought him a new trilby with the tiniest of blue feathers tucked into the band at the crown. He was clinging to her as though she was his mother, his head resting sleepily on her shoulder, buckling the brim of his hat. Often she glanced across the room to where O'Hara stood with his arm about Babs Osborne.

Bunny brought Meredith a plate of sandwiches; he waved them aside. Stella said she wasn't hungry either. 'I can't eat when I'm with you,' she told Meredith. 'I'd be sick. It's a compliment really.'

'I've known better ones,' he said. He seemed amused.

'I don't want anything to get in the way. Not sausage rolls or cheesy biscuits or anything. I want to listen.'

'I'm not sure I've got anything to say,' he said, and closed his eyes, his foot jogging up and down in time to the beat of the dance band on the gramophone. She studied the reflections on the wall as the lights of the Golden Dragon flashed blue and pink across the street.

'I knew it would be like this,' she said. 'I just knew.' She wasn't really talking to him; she thought he had dozed off.

He said, 'This isn't my room. I live at the back, over-looking the side of the church.'

'My grandfather played the organ there,' she told him. 'When Clara Butt gave song recitals.' She looked up and saw O'Hara staring at her over Babs Osborne's heaving shoulders. 'Miss Osborne is crying again,' she said, and asked, aggrieved, 'Why did you stop talking to me? Why didn't you want me to take notes anymore?'

'Oh, that,' Meredith said, opening his eyes. 'That was Rose, not me. You put the wind up her with that crucifix down your sock. She felt I was an undesirable influence, you coming from Methodist stock.'

She thought she had never seen anything so delicate as

his left eyelid quivering above the green ball of his eye, nor anything so vivid as the scarlet spots spattering the bow of his tie. On the wall behind him there was a picture of a stag lowering its antlers on a rocky promontory beneath puffy clouds. She lost concentration for a moment and the stag slipped from its frame and glided along the picture rail.

'Look,' she heard him say, 'I'm sorry if I've made you unhappy, but I'm not for you.'

'Do you mean you think you're too religious?' she asked.

'Something like that,' he said, and she fell sideways onto his lap and shut her eyes against the whirling room, her cheek stuck to the little glass circle of the monocle balanced on his chest.

She woke in a strange room, facing a dressing-table with a scarf just like Geoffrey's draped over the mirror. There was a tin ashtray on the bedside table and a framed photograph of two men in bathing costumes, linking arms on a pebbled beach. One of them was Meredith. She jumped up in a panic, terrified at being late home.

Meredith was still in the parlour, and Bunny. They were sitting on either side of a dying fire. Bunny said he would see her home.

'I don't need seeing,' she said. 'I'm perfectly capable of walking round the corner on my own.' She was already moving towards the door. She didn't say goodnight to Meredith. He had upset her although she couldn't remember in what way.

She had never been out alone at such an hour. The trams had stopped running and the sodium lights burned in the empty streets. She fully expected the basement door to be bolted.

Bunny followed at a discreet distance. He had telephoned Uncle Vernon before midnight to explain that Rose Lipman had insisted on Stella being present at a small celebration given by the Board of Governors.

10

THREE DAYS BEFORE CHRISTMAS VERNON WAS
brushing down the front steps when he saw Meredith crossing the end of the street. He would have ducked inside—
he was in his working clothes with not even a stud to his
shirt—but Meredith was already calling out a greeting and
advancing towards him.

They shook hands. 'My dear man,' said Meredith. 'Not
bad news, I hope.'

'Just the wireless,' Vernon said, taking a polishing cloth
from his pocket and dabbing at his eyes. They listened as
from the cellar below came the strains of a deep male voice
singing a sentimental ballad. 'It's to do with the low notes.
They always set me off. I first noticed it in the army when
music was compulsory.'

Meredith nodded in sympathy. They both gazed
thoughtfully along the wide, grey steet lined with blackened houses to where the unfinished transept of the rose-
pink cathedral smudged the high white sky. 'Over the dark
still silence,' quavered Vernon, singing along with the wireless, and was seized with a bout of coughing.

'That reminds me,' said Meredith. 'Is young Stella bron-
chial by any chance?'

"She is and she isn't,' Vernon said. 'I mean she's got the usual amount of congestion, but in her case it's aggravated by temperament, if you follow me.'

'I merely ask because last night she was unable to hold the torch steady. It was just before Peter enters and the night lights blow out. I take it you've seen the play?'

'What night lights?' asked Vernon.

'In the nursery scene. Fortunately the coughing didn't really matter so far as Tinkerbell was concerned . . . the light is supposed to flash erratically . . . but the noise was rather off-putting. Bunny's put a supply of cough drops in the prompt corner. I just wondered if there was anything radically wrong . . .'

'There's nothing wrong with her lungs, if that's what you mean,' Vernon said. 'We've had her X-rayed and she's sound as a bell.'

'That's all right then,' said Meredith.

'I'd better reimburse you for the sweets,' Vernon insisted, in a tight unfriendly voice. Clearly something other than the bass notes on the wireless niggled him.

In the end Meredith was forced to accept the three-pence thrust into his palm. Taken aback, he mentioned the football match to be fought on New Year's Day between the Repertory company and the pantomime cast of *Treasure Island* appearing at the Empire.

'I haven't got the wind,' said Vernon. 'My kicking days are over.' Meredith explained it was touch-line supporters they were after rather than players. A charabanc would be leaving from Williamson Square at ten o'clock. 'Do come,' he urged. 'It would be lovely to have you with us.'

An Awfully Big Adventure

'I'll think about it,' said Vernon, and he stumped up the steps with his polishing cloth and rubbed vigorously at the lion's-head knocker of the door.

He waited until Meredith had turned the corner before going downstairs to put on his Sunday overcoat. Though all but one of the travellers had decamped for Christmas, he didn't care to be seen improperly dressed in the hall. He ran back upstairs to telephone Harcourt.

'I shouldn't have insisted on him taking the threepence, should I?' he said.

'It depends on his tone of voice,' said Harcourt. 'Was he annoyed or genuinely anxious?'

'You didn't see her, did you?' accused Vernon. 'You never got there . . .'

'We were given a refund,' protested Harcourt. 'I can hardly be blamed if the production was cancelled.'

'The Board of Governors have noticed her,' said Vernon. 'She's been singled out.'

'There you are then. There's nothing to worry about.'

'All the same,' said Vernon. 'Life has a nasty habit of repeating itself.' He stood with his shoulder pressed against the wall, his gaze fixed on the fanlight. Just then the boom of the one o'clock gun echoed across the river; the glass flushed crimson as the neon sign flashed above the door. He thought of the flares bursting like orange plums in the soot-black night, illuminating the trucks, the humped tanks, the upflung arms of waking men shielding their eyes from the glare. He said, 'I may have mentioned I saw service in the desert . . .'

'Once or twice,' admitted Harcourt.

'There was one particular evening when Jerry sent up a barrage of Verey lights. They were trying to find our position.'

'I remember you telling me,' Harcourt said.

'It was different for our Stella. In her case someone was all too willing to abandon her.'

'I don't quite follow your gist,' said Harcourt.

Vernon remained silent for perhaps half a minute. 'No,' he said, at last. 'It's not easy.'

Just then Lily shouted up from the basement to complain that the kitchen range was smoking again. 'I blame next door,' Vernon told Harcourt. 'They eat different food. It's bound to affect the chimney.'

'Would you like me to accompany you?' Harcourt asked. 'To the match?'

Vernon was staggered. Never once had his supplier suggested they should meet socially. Over the years they had attended the same victuallers' functions, and on every occasion Harcourt had kept very much to his own table. He had raised his glass civilly enough in recognition of Vernon's presence whenever their eyes had met across the floral displays, and he had always been very effusive if they chanced to meet in the queue for the cloakroom or on the pavement outside the State Restaurant, but he had held his distance in mixed company, had never introduced him, for instance, to Mrs Harcourt. Not that she was anything to write home about, in spite of coming from the Wirral.

'Much obliged for the offer,' Vernon said, 'but I shan't go. The wife's brother is coming up for the festivities.'

He was cock-a-hoop when he recounted this part of

the conversation to Lily. 'The nerve of it,' he crowed. 'Muscling in on a theatrical invitation. It just shows you how pushy the educated classes can be when they smell an advantage.'

He didn't tell Stella he had been asked to the football match. She too had received an invitation, to a supper dance at Reece's Grill Room on Christmas Eve. Originally St Ives had intended a foursome consisting of himself and Dotty, Babs Osborne and her elusive foreigner. Incapacitated as he now was and about to go off to stay with his mother in Weston-super-Mare, St Ives had sold the tickets to Desmond Fairchild. The party had since grown and extra tickets had been bought. The company had clubbed together to pay for her and Geoffrey. It was a sort of Christmas present.

'That was kind, wasn't it?' said Lily. 'I hope you thanked them.'

'We run errands for them all day long,' Stella retorted. 'I don't have to go overboard with delight.'

'Is Geoffrey your partner then?' asked Lily. She was smiling, participating at second hand in the evening to come.

'No, he isn't,' snapped Stella. She wanted Lily to stop talking. It was spoiling things, this building up of expectations.

'Well, who is?' said Lily. 'You'll need a partner.'

'It's not that sort of do. We're not in couples. Grace Bird is an abandoned wife and Babs's Stanislaus has jilted her. Not that she accepts it. She keeps ringing him and sending him presents.'

Lily said Babs was a foolish girl. No man liked to be chased. She should buy herself a new frock and set her cap at someone else. That would soon bring this Stan chap running.

'Why would it?' asked Stella. 'If he doesn't want her?'

'He doesn't want her,' squealed Lily, 'because he's got her. He'd soon change his tune if he thought she'd lost interest. They're all the same. You tell her from me.'

Stella tried to imagine a younger Lily giving Uncle Vernon cause for jealousy. It wasn't possible. The real Lily sat opposite, her too brightly-coloured hair set in stiff waves about her faded face.

'Hasn't your Mr Potter got a young lady?' persisted Lily. 'It stands to reason a man like that would have a partner.'

'Shut up,' Stella shouted. 'Not everybody needs propping up, you know. Not everybody wants . . .' and trailed into silence, for Lily's eyelids were now fluttering, holding back offended tears. Stella jumped up and made a clattering show of stacking the supper plates onto a tray.

Alone in her room, struggling into her ice-cold night-gown, she felt ashamed. It was unjust of her to disregard those thumb-sucking years in which Lily had held her close. In the end everyone expected a return on love, demanded a rebate of gratitude or respect. It was no different from collecting the deposit on lemonade bottles. She should have given Lily a cuddle.

Instead she got into bed. I have my whole life in front of me, she thought. I can't be hamstrung by sentiment.

*

Stella had planned to sit next to Meredith at the Christmas Eve party, but Geoffrey got there first. It was her own fault. Not wanting anyone to see her dress from behind—the hem had come undone and she wasn't wearing stockings—she had hung back as they came through the doors of the Grill Room.

The head waiter made a servile fuss when they arrived and begged permission for a photograph to be taken for publicity purposes. Then Dotty Blundell, who a moment before had drooped under the weight of her leopard-skin coat, flung back her shoulders and lowering her chin gave a peek-a-boo smile. John Harbour, as if looking into a mirror, leaned chummily against Babs Osborne and stared adoringly at the camera. Stella was coughing when the flash bulb went off.

The dance floor, wreathed in blue smoke, was crowded with revellers foxtrotting to the magnified beat of the paper-hatted band perspiring beneath a trembling canopy of holly boughs and mistletoe. An army of waiters carrying silver-plated dishes barged back and forth through the swing doors of the kitchens. The restaurant was so packed that there weren't enough chairs, and somehow Geoffrey squeezed in between Stella and Meredith. He squatted on his haunches, his pug nose on a level with the table. 'I can't go on like this,' he said, shouting to make himself heard. 'We have to talk.'

'Absolutely,' Meredith replied. 'Couldn't agree more.'

And fitting his monocle beneath the bone of his eye he studied the menu.

'He's thinking of going into business,' Stella said. 'His father would like it.' Meredith didn't respond. Geoffrey crouched at his knee like a faithful dog. Another chair was fetched from the store-room and Stella was forced to make a space for it. She could have throttled Geoffrey, wriggling in where he wasn't wanted.

Bunny was there under duress. 'I gain no pleasure from that sort of entertainment,' he had protested earlier to Meredith. 'I don't dance, and neither do you. We shall be spectres at the feast.'

'Bear with me,' Meredith had said. 'It may well turn out to be diverting.'

At eleven o'clock, fifteen minutes after being shown to their table, Bunny threatened to leave. He detested turkey and there was nothing else he fancied apart from the chocolate gâteau. Meredith told him to stop moaning and ordered him a double portion of cake as a main course. 'He's a sick man,' he informed the waiter. 'They couldn't get all the shrapnel out.' Bunny saw the joke. He was wearing a clean shirt and a tartan tie under a crumpled blazer whose buttons were missing; he began to laugh and quantities of cigarette ash spilled from his clothing and speckled the tablecloth.

Stella chose fish and regretted it. She kept getting bones in her mouth and each time she took one out O'Hara appeared to be looking in her direction. If it would have caught Meredith's attention she wouldn't have minded a bone lodging in her gullet, but then there was always the risk he might think she was merely coughing—she could choke for nothing. Presently she stopped eating and hid the fish under a heap of Brussels sprouts. Geoffrey, the food untouched on his plate, sat sideways on his chair, bellowing into Meredith's ear. She sat back and freed her hair from the collar of her frock. 'My dear boy,' she heard Meredith say, 'you're far too sensitive.'

O'Hara, watching Stella, was disconcerted by the wave of tenderness evoked by the sight of her bright hair rippling like a flag against the dark wall. He was half-heartedly involved in a discussion on Mary Deare, who at this moment was speeding in a hired car towards Manchester to spend Christmas Day at the Midland Hotel with an un-named friend appearing in *The Tinder Box*. Mary had abrasions in her armpits, some of them serious, from wearing her flying harness next to her skin. The wardrobe had provided her with a vest of padded cotton, but for some reason she wouldn't wear it. Grace had seen the blisters.

'I bleed for her,' announced Harbour. 'Just think of it—she suffers agonies every time she flies.'

'She can't bear to carry an ounce more than her usual weight,' said Grace Bird. 'She dispensed with the vest because it made her feel larger than life. She's neurotic.'

'You're right,' cried Babs Osborne excitedly. 'Stanislaus said he knew people in the camps who experienced satisfaction when they started to waste. Stanislaus knew one woman who . . .'

'I'm sure this stuffing's off,' said Grace, and she impaled a lump on her fork and thrust it across the cloth for John Harbour to sniff at.

Stella, who for a miserable quarter of an hour had been contemplating going to the ladies' room and not coming back, was suddenly struck by the curiously fragmented nature of the group about the table. She had dreaded the moment when the food would be done with and the others would get up to dance, leaving her on her own at the table. Now she saw that all of them were alone, not least those who chatted so animatedly together. Contrary to what Lily might think, a twosome was an inaccurate indication of partnership. Dotty, apparently listening attentively to Desmond Fairchild, her hand on his arm, was looking at O'Hara. Even in the throes of laughing at some remark passed by Grace Bird, Bunny watched Geoffrey. John Harbour, confiding something important to Babs Osborne, kept glancing at Meredith. Babs didn't notice; she was staring straight ahead, dreaming of Stanislaus. Only Geoffrey, tugging at his hair, sniffing, thumping the tablecloth, could be said to be concentrating on the person beside him. He was demanding something of Meredith, that much was evident. The words 'unfair advantage' were used, and then Stella distinctly heard Geoffrey say, 'You're ruining my life.'

She was amazed at his ambition; he had given her to understand he wanted to give up the theatre. She nudged him in the ribs and hissed, 'Don't be such a twerp. You can't bully him into giving you better parts.'

'Mind your own business,' he shouted, turning on her quite violently. 'You don't know what you're talking about.'

Just then O'Hara rose from his chair and invited Stella

to dance. 'I'm no good at it,' she lied, and, pleased, struggled her way from the table and walked stiffly into his arms.

O'Hara wasn't a tall man. She didn't know the colour of his eyes because she had never looked into them. He was stocky and broad-shouldered and he had thick black eyebrows. Until now she hadn't taken much notice of him, so she couldn't say for certain whether he was handsome or not. There was a smear of yellow greasepaint on the collar of his shirt. His hand, clasping her own as he steered her about the floor, was somewhat cold.

At last Meredith was looking at her. I'm setting my cap at someone else, she thought, circling the room with her chin in the air.

By the time they returned to the table for the Christmas pudding John Harbour had moved and there was nowhere for her to sit except beside O'Hara. A woman came up with a red balloon and asked him to autograph it, and he took out a fountain pen and commenced a squeaky signature. The balloon burst as he scrawled the last letter. The woman said it didn't matter. They both hunted through the debris on the floor to find that shrivelled scrap bearing his name. O'Hara didn't ask Stella to dance again. He was too busy trying to restrain Babs Osborne from telephoning Stanislaus.

Half an hour later Meredith announced he'd had enough. Bunny and he were off to Midnight Mass. Stella hoped he might ask her to go with them but he didn't even say good-bye, not properly, let alone wish her a Merry Christmas. One minute he was at the table and the next he was threading his way between the dancers, leaving Geoffrey asleep with his cheek resting on a bread roll, bits of tinsel glittering in his hair.

'Shall I give you a lift home on my motorbike?' O'Hara asked, and Stella accepted at once, almost running out of the restaurant, scarcely bothering to wave a farewell to the others who were now giddily swaying across the dance floor. Desmond Fairchild, paddling through the spotlights, his trousers rolled up to his hairy knees, shouted something at her. She pretended not to notice. All that mattered was that she should catch up with Meredith.

O'Hara took a long time to kick-start the motorbike from the kerb. 'Which way?' he asked, when at last the engine sputtered into life, and she directed him the wrong way round so that they might overtake and confront the trio lurching towards Midnight Mass.

She shouted contradictory commands. 'Faster, faster,' she ordered, as they puttered up Brownlow Hill, empty of Meredith. 'Not so fast,' she cried as they thundered along Rodney Street. She didn't care what O'Hara thought. She didn't care about anything; she just wanted Meredith to see her on the back of the Prince's white charger. Perhaps then, when he realised he was in danger of losing her, he and O'Hara would exchange a hostile, challenging glance. If looks could kill, she thought, clinging to O'Hara's leather-clad waist, the river wind whipping her hair into her eyes.

She had almost given up hope when she saw Meredith arm in arm with Grace and Bunny stepping off the kerb outside the Women's Hospital. 'Slower, slower,' she screamed over O'Hara's shoulder, fearful they might pass unnoticed.

Bunny and Grace saw her, she was sure. Startled, Bunny stepped backwards, dragging Meredith with him. Grace swung her handbag in recognition, and a ball of wool jerked out and fell to the gutter. Stella kept her arm in the air, waving, waving long after O'Hara had swerved the motorcycle round the corner.

She wouldn't let him take her to the Aber House Hotel. Instead she made him stop in the next street; she didn't want Uncle Vernon storming up the basement steps and putting his oar in. 'I'll make you a cup of tea,' offered O'Hara. 'I only live two doors up.'

'If you like,' Stella agreed. 'It's interesting to see how other people live.'

When she saw she was disconcerted. The room was tidy enough, after a fashion, but there was nothing of value on the mantelpiece and not one stick of furniture that wouldn't have been better employed on a bonfire. She was surprised he lived so poorly, him being a successful man. 'It isn't very salubrious, is it?' she said, eyeing the scuffed skirting-board, the mushroom growths on the wall.

'I was happy here once,' he told her.

There was nowhere to sit but on the narrow bed beside the fireplace.

'I can smell something,' Stella said. 'I've a very good nose for smells.'

He apologised for the damp and she shook her head. 'I know about that sort of smell. It's sweet. This is different.' She sat there wrinkling her nose, trying to identify what it was. 'Turpentine,' she cried at last. 'Turpentine and linseed oil.'

He was impressed and proceeded to tell her about Keeley, recalling some inflammable occasion on which Keeley had set fire to something or someone. Her jaw ached with smiling her appreciation. What fun they'd had, he concluded.

'Where is he now?' she asked, thinking he was possibly behind bars.

'I lost touch with him when he joined the Air Force. I'm not entirely convinced he survived. I've a painting of his at home, of this room with me standing by the door. I'm very fond of it.'

'Mr Potter knows about paintings. He took me round the Walker Art Gallery. He likes the religious ones best.'

'He would,' said O'Hara.

She could tell there was something bothering him. He wasn't quite comfortable with her. He was looking at her intently, as if he expected she might do something surprising, like flying up the chimney.

Suddenly he kissed her. She opened her lips obediently and remained perfectly still. When he let her go she wiped her mouth on her sleeve.

He said, 'Perhaps I ought to take you home.' He sounded grumpy.

'I don't mind staying if it's all the same to you,' she said. It had to happen sometime and now was as good a time as any. She wanted to get it over with.

It was unusual, that was for sure. She felt a certain sad excitement, a little discomfort and much embarrassment, the latter concerned with the removal of clothing. *I am dying, Egypt, dying,* her mind gabbled when Dotty Blundell's brassière fell to the dusty floor. She hadn't been prepared for the way poetry came into this fitting together of parts, *Shall I believe that unsubstantial Death is amorous, and that the lean abhorrèd monster keeps Thee here in dark to be his paramour,* she recited in her head, as O'Hara climbed on top and humped her beneath the rude unshaded bulb. Not that O'Hara was either lean or a monster. 'Stella Maris,' he muttered against her hair, and jumped away like a fish leaping on a bank.

When it appeared to be over—he'd stopped breathing so heavily and lay with his eyes closed—she asked him who Stella Maris was.

'Did I say that?' he said, and sat up and combed his hair. 'I knew someone of that name a long time ago. It means Star of the Sea.'

'Stella Maris,' she repeated. 'It's nice.'

'It wasn't her real name,' he said. 'Just something she made up.'

She was staring somewhat scornfully at his plump shoulders. He put on his shirt and suggested she should wash herself at the sink. She refused; she'd had a bath the night before.

'You mustn't worry,' he said. 'I was very careful. I'm not an irresponsible man.'

She supposed he was thinking about babies. She wasn't bothered. If what she had done was a sin then it was only right she should be punished. 'No use crying over spilt milk,' she said. If she had weakened for a moment, to the

extent of uttering one soft word of forgiveness, of friendship, she might have burst into tears. Already in the expression of her eyes, the beginnings of her small, triumphant
smile, there was more than a touch of the martyr.

'Did you enjoy it?' he asked, not looking at her.

'Not really,' she admitted. 'I expect there's a knack to
it. It's very intimate, isn't it?'

He insisted on walking her home but she ran off at the
corner. He wasn't pleased with himself. Whatever mo-
mentary spasm of pleasure he had experienced was now
forgotten. He was also more than a little scandalised at the
girl's matter-of-fact acceptance of what had happened. She
hadn't wept or clung to him, demanded to know what he
felt about her, uttered those naive and sweetly foolish
declarations of undying love expected of a young girl
whose virgnity had just been taken. He was fairly certain
she had no idea of how gentle he had been, how thoughtful.
One way and another he felt let down.

Stella didn't go home, not right away. Instead she walked
as fast as she could towards the river, past the mean little
houses below the cathedral. She almost choked on the
stench of damp grain blowing up the hill.

There was a man in the telephone box outside the Mission Hall. She crouched in the shadows of the porch and
watched the blurred lights of a Christmas tree winking in
the first-floor room of a house opposite. A little girl carrying either a doll or a child walked back and forth behind
the windows.

It was cold in the street. The chemical clouds curdled

above the black top-hats of the chimney stacks. From the dock road came a steady rumble of traffic and the heartbeat of machinery as the sugar-refinery pumped in the fiery darkness. At last the man staggered out, a string of sausages slung about his neck.

She pressed button A and heard Mother's voice; she felt shy. She had meant to confide that she, too, was a seduced woman; yet when it came to it she couldn't find the correct words. All the poetry had dribbled out of her. She wished Mother a Happy Christmas, her eyes fixed on the child across the road and that silhouette of Mr Punch who now appeared with raised and menacing fist.

Mother responded in the usual way.

11

AT THE MATINEE ON BOXING DAY O'HARA, dragging a reluctant Nana by the collar, made his exit as Mr Darling and raced upstairs to transform himself into Captain Hook. On his return Geoffrey should have been waiting in the wings to assist him into his pirate coat—the hook attached to the sleeve rendered it cumbersome. He wasn't there. The child who played Tootles stood on a chair and helped him instead. It was a breach of discipline, Geoffrey being absent.

During the second interval Geoffrey apologised, giving the excuse that one of the battens of the hollow trees had worked itself loose and that at the last moment Bunny had required him to fix it more securely into its brace. But then at the evening performance he again went missing.

This time Stella was there to heave O'Hara into the coat. He said, 'Did you have a good Christmas?', and not looking at him she thanked him for asking and replied that it had been quiet but nice.

She was being polite. Uncle Vernon, goaded by the presence of the traveller with the skin grafts, had ruined the festive meal with recollections of his march across France and an encounter in a partially demolished farmhouse outside Lille with a white-haired woman of thirty who as a small child had suffered atrocities in the First World War. German officers—second-line supply men—searching for food and told there was none had wrenched her from her mother's arms and, dumping her in the washing boiler on the kitchen stove, threatened to cook and eat her.

On hearing the story Lily had retired to bed with a headache leaving Stella to do the washing-up. The traveller had dried the dishes. Tears ran down his cheeks, but that was because his eyes couldn't blink. Uncle Vernon, wearing a paper crown jerked from a cracker, had nodded off in his armchair listening to a choral mass on the Third Programme.

Stella was in the prompt corner wielding her torch when O'Hara made his second exit. He loitered in the wings, although usually he sat in his dressing-room until the curtain rose on the Mermaid's Lagoon. He noticed she was wearing a string of cheap pearls about her neck. On stage the First Twin had sighted the white bird and was declaiming, 'See it comes, the Wendy,' and Tootles, pointing at the gossamer light sailing across the painted trees, called out, 'Tink is trying to hurt the Wendy.' A child in the audience shouted a timid warning. Then Stella, responding to a signal from Bunny, swung her hand-bell.

'Someone's been splashing out at Woolworths,' said O'Hara, tapping with his hook at the pearls. In the half-darkness his face with its rouged lips, its black cross stamped on the cheekbone, was ghastly.

'Quiet please,' hissed Bunny.

Frowning, O'Hara inched open the pass door and tiptoed into the prop-room. He was annoyed at being caught in the wrong.

George rolled him a cigarette. 'Word in your ear,' he said. 'Someone should keep a weather eye on young Geoffrey.'

'He's let me down twice today,' O'Hara said. 'What's up with him?'

'No disrespect intended, Captain,' said George. 'But you'd best work it out for yourself.'

After the curtain call O'Hara asked Stella if she wanted a lift home on his motor-cycle. 'If you like,' she said. She kept him waiting and when she finally emerged from the stage door he had been waylaid by Freddie Reynalde. She walked past without looking at them.

'What about a drink?' suggested Freddie.

O'Hara said he couldn't face Potter.

'We don't have to go to the Oyster Bar.'

'Another time, old chap. I'm bushed.'

'I can see that,' Freddie said, and they both watched the girl trudging towards the corner.

O'Hara caught up with Stella at the bottom of the hill. She told him to go on ahead, that she didn't want a ride.

'Why not?' he asked.

'I just don't,' she said. 'My uncle wouldn't like it.' He thought she meant she was going straight home and drove off with a sulky smile.

He was surprised when she rapped on the basement window. Entering, she circled the room, her expression hostile. He lit the gas-fire and made her kneel in front of

it to warm herself. 'I'm not stopping,' she said, teeth chattering. 'You ought to wrap up more,' he advised. 'Now
that it's winter. You've a terrible cough.' She protested
she'd rather freeze than wear the coat Lily had bought her.
It was too big and it had a fur collar.

'It sounds rather glamorous,' he said.

'That's as maybe,' she retorted. 'It's too much trouble.
You have to paint your face if you wear a fur. It draws
attention.'

He found himself involved in an argument about silver
wrapping-paper only serving to accentuate the paltriness
of a gift. It was best, she said, to encase cheap goods in
brown paper. Shaken, he imagined she was feeling guilty
at having given herself so easily. He heard himself saying
it was surely the thought that counted, and was astonished
at the banal words that hurtled from his mouth. She
crouched on the lino, her face flushed from the fire, fin-
gering that string of Christmas cracker beads.

He asked who had given her them, and she said they
were a present from her mother. He apologised for having
suggested they were bought at Woolworths. She looked
at him without blinking and said they probably had been.
That was why her mother hadn't wrapped them up but had
left them on her pillow twined around a single rose.

'What a lovely thing to do,' he remarked and, appalled
at his patronising tone, told her that her ears should have
been burning on Christmas Day. Several of the company
had dined at the Adelphi Hotel and during the meal Dotty
Blundell had sung her praises. Dotty considered her per-

formance as Ptolemy exceptional for someone so inex-
perienced. 'I'm devastated I missed it,' he said. 'Did you
enjoy doing it?'

'Was Mr Potter with you?' she asked.

'He and Bunny went to an aunt in Hoylake. You should
have played Cleopatra, you know. You're the right age.
By all accounts Babs was miscast.'

'Has Bunny got an auntie in Hoylake?'

'Bunny's from the South,' he said. 'Potter's the local boy.'

She stared at him in disbelief, as though suspecting him
of flattery. 'You could have played it,' he insisted. 'Dotty
isn't the only one who thinks you're talented. But you have
to look after yourself a bit more, take a little more trouble
with your appearance.'

'Mr Potter's never from Liverpool.'

'Of course he is,' he said. 'His mother attended the same
elementary school as Rose.'

Still she stared at him, hugging her knees. 'Acting,' he
continued, 'is an extremely physical profession. It's not
enough to know how to speak the lines. There's breathing
and stamina and control of the body. One has to stand
properly, take care of one's eyes, one's skin. Even a painting by Rubens can be enhanced by the correct frame.'

'Did Dotty tell you about my boil?' she said.

Exasperated, he took her into his arms to shut her up.
She was so near to him that he had to close his eyes.

Afterwards she was more friendly. He put a record on
the gramophone and she sat on his lap, wrapped in a blanket, and lolled affectionately against his shoulder. She said

she thought she was beginning to get the hang of it. It was no different from learning the piano or the ukulele; it just needed practice.

He rocked her in time to the music, tugging sleepily at the pearls about her throat. As if reciting endearments, she whispered into his ear. 'You don't want to take too much notice of anything I tell you. Sometimes I say whatever comes into my head. It's why Uncle Vernon wanted me to go on the stage.'

'What's that supposed to mean?' he asked, not really bothered.

'I play-act,' she said. 'I always have. I mourn people in my head. I go to funerals and chuck earth. Sometimes I have to choose who I'm going to bury. I like to rehearse the bad things so that I'll know how to behave when they really happen.'

'Silly goose,' he murmured fondly, scarcely listening.

'It's on account of my background,' she said, and shivered.

He offered to buy her a coat. She could choose it for herself—money was no object. She jumped from his lap and struggled into her clothes. In her haste to be gone she stuffed Dotty Blundell's brassière into the pocket of her overalls.

'For God's sake,' he cried. 'What did I say?'

She wouldn't speak to him and was out of the door in an instant. He thought of following her and then changed his mind; he was too old for that sort of gesture. Rattled, he fell back onto the truckle-bed in a welter of trousers.

*

Vernon went on the tram to the football match. He'd decided it was best to keep out of Stella's way until he was actually at the field. With any luck she mightn't even spot him. There was an awkward moment at the breakfast-table when she asked him why he was wearing his Sunday suit.

'None of your business,' he told her and, gritting his teeth, refrained from commenting on her own mode of dress.

'And *she's* ashamed of me,' he fumed to Lily, when Stella had at last left the house. 'It's a wonder she's not mistaken for a boilerman. If I had my way I'd set fire to those blasted overalls.'

'It's a phase,' soothed Lily. 'She's trying to hide herself.'

O'Hara waited for Stella outside the theatre. A procession of *Treasure Island* pirates carrying cardboard boxes bulging with beer bottles were already noisily boarding the coach. Bunny, unshaven, stood at the kerb with the stage manager of the Empire. He said worriedly, 'I hope you're going to keep an eye on that lot. We don't want any injuries.'

'Don't talk soft,' said the manager. 'They're mostly chorus boys.'

The celebrated comedian who was playing Long John Silver made a brief appearance in a chauffeur-driven car.

'I'm on my way, playmates,' he called, winding down the window to show his melancholy face. He was eating a bacon sandwich and hurled the crusts into the gutter as the car drove off.

Stella came up the street with Geoffrey and walked straight past O'Hara. She clung on to Geoffrey's coat as he hauled himself onto the coach. Just then Dotty turned the corner arm in arm with Desmond Fairchild. She stopped and jabbed at O'Hara's machine with her umbrella. 'That bloody bike,' she said, although she knew it wasn't the same one.

Ignoring her O'Hara ran up and down the pavement waving his arms, trying to attract Stella's attention. He was fairly certain she had seen him. Humiliated, he returned to his motor-cycle and, mounting the saddle, stabbed the toe of his flying boot furiously against the starter pedal. Trailed by a cloud of exhaust fumes, he accelerated up the road.

All the way to the football ground he thought about her. Every evening since Boxing Night she had come to his basement-room and allowed him to make love to her.

'You're sure you like doing this, aren't you?' he had asked her in the darkness. 'I'm not making you do something you don't want to do?'

'Nobody makes me do anything I don't want to do,' she assured him. Yet when he saw her the next day and attempted to speak to her she told him to leave her alone and ran off into the prop-room.

She had confided she was in love with someone else, but he didn't believe her. It wasn't possible she was attached to young Geoffrey—whenever she mentioned him her voice had an edge of contempt. He couldn't fathom why she was so anxious that no one else should know of his interest in her. All the women he had ever known had wanted to flaunt their possession of him, however fleeting.

He had let slip he was married. He'd begun to tell her an anecdote about the time he'd been trying out some play in Brighton when he'd very nearly missed the curtain because he'd accidently locked himself in his hotel-room, and how if it hadn't been for his wife—realising his blunder he broke off and wanted to know if she minded his being married. 'Why should I?' Stella had answered. 'People of your age usually are.'

He had laughed, and felt unreasonably hurt. A short time later he couldn't prevent himself from asking whether she didn't love him just a little. 'I've told you,' she said, 'I love someone else.'

'But you don't do this with him, do you?' he demanded, straddling her on the lumpy bed and thrusting into her.

'What's that got to do with it,' she had said, screwing up her face in concentration.

For all his worldliness he was shocked. He was afraid she was becoming corrupt. He had only to suggest she lift her hips a fraction higher or arch her back rather more sharply for her to comply at once. She began to add certain embellishments of her own. On their third night she ordered him quite roughly to bring his legs closer together and found a way of rubbing herself against his knee while sucking at his neck that made him shudder.

The following day he bought her a bunch of violets and dropped them on her lap as she sat in the prompt corner. She turned on him and hissed that Bunny was watching. When he came off stage the violets had been kicked into the wings, stamped on by Tiger Lily's Redskins.

He couldn't make her out, or himself for that matter. What had started as an unimportant if rather shameful seduction had become something altogether more painful. He had lost his heart and was in danger of losing his head.

The football ground was at the back of a churchyard in the suburbs. There was a ramshackle club-house with its roof falling in and a rickety stand which rocked in the wind. Already fifty or more spectators, mostly old men and young lads, stood on the touchline stamping their feet to keep warm.

Shortly three carloads of young women arrived, followed by the limousine carring Long John Silver. The girls tumbled out and began to teeter up the path towards the field. There was a glitter of frost on the patchy grass and a cold white sun high above the poplar trees beyond the boundary wall of the cemetery. Unsuitably dressed and squealing in the nippy air, the girls ran round like chickens before fleeing back to the cars. The comedian waited where he was, swigging from his hip flask.

When the coach arrived it took some time to organise the teams. Having inspected the club-house Bunny pronounced it unsafe. Even the wooden steps leading up to the door were rotten.

'Back, back,' he cried, as the pirates ran towards him.

'Think of your ankles, boys,' shouted the stage-manager of the Empire Theatre, standing his ground and shooing them away.

The girls, coaxed from the cars and persuaded to sit on the bottom row of the stand, were heaped with the players' coats and scarves and warned not to fidget. The stand swayed alarmingly under their weight and one or two screamed nervously.

Vernon was bewildered at first. The teams weren't even dressed properly. Many of the players refused to get into shorts, and the Empire goalie wore cricket pads over striped long-johns. The celebrated comedian had a cigar clamped in his mouth. His chauffeur kept pace with him on the sideline, carrying a flask which glinted in the chilly sunlight. It was obvious it wasn't going to be a serious game.

Vernon regretted giving Harcourt the cold shoulder; he would have been someone to laugh with. He recognised no one apart from Stella and Potter. Stella stood in the middle of the field talking to the only chap properly attired in shorts and jersey. He had his hand on her arm and was evidently asking her to do something. Whatever it was, she wan't amenable. Vernon was ashamed of her. She wore a naval greatcoat with brass buttons and some sort of goggles on her head. The coat was far too large for her and trailed the ground as she stalked off; she didn't bother to hitch it up.

Just before the whistle blew Vernon thought she had seen him; at any rate she was looking in his direction. He half raised his arm to draw her attention, and thought better of it. There was no rush. She'd probably join him later. If he was careful she might even allow him to travel back with her on the coach.

Meredith acted as referee. Stella was disappointed he wouldn't be taking a more active part. She knew little about football, but it was immediately obvious even to her that

Geoffrey and O'Hara were superior to the rest of the field. On the coach Geoffrey had stared morosely out of the window; now he stormed along the wing with ferocious determination. Within the first minute he scored a goal, and another a quarter of an hour later. He didn't seem particularly pleased with himself even though he was patted enthusiastically on the back by the rest of his team and applauded by the spectators.

Much of the game took place in mid-field, or in front of the *Treasure Island* goal, and Meredith had his back to Stella most of the time. She had gone to stand at the cemetery end after spotting Uncle Vernon on the touch-line in front of the club-house.

Soon she grew bored with watching and wandered away down the path towards the road. There was a hearse parked at the kerb outside the church and a man in a black bowler hat polishing the bodywork with a yellow duster. 'They've begun,' he said, and she nodded and quickened her step obediently.

The door made a terrible creaking sound when she pushed it open. She saw a coffin on trestles below the altar steps and a vicar in a white surplice with his back to the aisle. The window behind the altar had been replaced with a piece of board across which someone had scrawled in black paint 'This side up'. A single light burned unshaded above the communion table, turning the scene into a badly lit play. She would have backed out again if the mourners, disturbed by the noise of the door, hadn't swivelled round to look at her. There were three of them, two women and a man, all old and white-haired, each with a shepherd's crook of a walking-stick propped against the pew in front. There was no one else there save for a hidden organist who presently began to thunder an untuneful hymn.

It was a short service. The church was so vast and empty that the vicar's words rolled away into the gloom. One of the old ladies blew her nose and the explosion echoed round the walls to fade like the barking of a dog.

Stella pretended it was Uncle Vernon in the coffin. She concentrated but felt nothing. Dying wouldn't be such an awfully big adventure for Uncle Vernon—he was too old. She substituted Meredith. Still she couldn't feel sad; if anything she was angry at his deceitful slipping away. She imagined herself lying there, the life gone from her. Uncle Vernon and Meredith were weeping. She was beginning to feel quite mournful when she remembered that Meredith was a Catholic and wouldn't be allowed in the church.

The door behind her cranked open. She turned and saw the man in the bowler. He looked beyond her and lifted one finger in a beckoning gesture. Four undertaker's men slid out of the shadows of the vestry and, picking up the coffin, bore it up the aisle. The vicar paced behind, holding his prayer book, his hair floating up and down in the draught from the door. Stella would have fled if she hadn't thought it sacreligious to race ahead of the dead. She stood with closed eyes, listening to the measured footsteps.

When she opened them again one of the elderly ladies had drawn level with her. Her stick slithering on the flag-stones, the old woman halted, swaying. Stella put a hand under her elbow to support her. Together they tottered to the door. As they came out onto the path a muffled roar sounded from the football pitch.

'Thank you for coming,' the old woman said. 'He would have been pleased.'

When the coffin had been lowered into the hole and the suitable words uttered, the vicar searched for Stella's hand in the overlong sleeve of O'Hara's coat.

'Did you know the deceased well?' he asked.

'Yes and no,' she said.

'Put your trust in the resurrection,' he told her, and hurried away, face purple with the cold.

Stella walked to the poplar-trees and peered over the wall into the field. She saw a figure lying on the ground and O'Hara holding Geoffrey's arms behind his back. Everybody was shouting.

*

O'Hara and Freddie Reynalde dragged Geoffrey from the pitch and marched him out of sight behind the club-house. Exhorting him to breathe deeply they paraded him up and down beside the wire fence. He was trembling and so drenched in sweat that his hair lay like streaks of black paint upon his forehead. In bursts he wept, angrily.

The spectators began to leave the field. Chivvying his players into their coats and scarves, the Empire stage-manager herded them back to the coach. Within Dotty's hearing a home pirate remarked that he thought it had all been a storm in a teacup. She prodded him fiercely in the buttocks with the tip of her brolly, accusing him of disloyalty.

'Nothing excuses violence,' she shouted. 'It was a disgraceful outburst.'

The pirate looked unrepentant. Desmond Fairchild gave him a sympathetic wink.

Meredith sat on the grass with his chin tilted to the sky as if sunbathing. Bunny waved aside the comedian's offer of a little nip from the hip flask.

'It might do more harm than good,' he said, alarmed at the amount of blood running down Meredith's face.

'For God's sake,' choked Meredith, 'I've a nose-bleed not a stomach wound.'

'You were knocked out,' Bunny protested.

'I fainted,' corrected Meredith. 'The pain was excruciating.'

'You're going to have to get rid of dear Geoffrey,' cried John Harbour, flushed with excitement. 'He shouldn't be allowed to get away with such vile behaviour. You must tell Rose to send him packing.'

'What a brilliant idea,' said Meredith. 'Just the ticket when you think about it.' He got to his feet and pushed Harbour contemptuously aside. 'My coat,' he told Bunny. 'I want my coat.'

Harbour, having scanned the field for Geoffrey—he had some notion of rushing him from the rear and felling him with a rabbit-chop—ran off to compare notes with Dotty and the others.

Meredith was unthreading his monocle from its blood-stained ribbon when Vernon approached. Together they strode toward the path. 'I like these sort of mornings,' said Vernon. 'A hint of frost, a touch of sunlight.'

'It's invigorating, isn't it?' agreed Meredith. 'A man can stand upright.'

Vernon was nodding his assent when he tripped. For an instant, startled by that snapping sound, he thought he had trodden on a twig. He fell down, felled by a white bolt of agony.

'Stella,' he cried out, 'where's our Stella?'

Stella watched from behind the poplars as the comedian's limousine bumped up the path to where Vernon lay. She wanted to climb the wall and run forward to comfort him. He was quite close. His trouser-leg had fallen back, exposing the elasticated suspender circling his diamond-mottled calf. 'Stella,' he called again, as if asking for the only person he needed. His hat tipped off and began to blow away in the wind. She closed her eyes and stuffed her fingers in her ears. She hummed a song in her head.

That evening, responding to a note from Desmond Fairchild, O'Hara went to Grace Bird's dressing-room at the quarter hour. Dotty and Babs were there.

'Look here, Squire,' said Desmond, 'we were wondering if you would have a word with Potter.'

'Geoffrey's behaviour was inexcusable,' Grace said. 'But it does seem like a cry for help. And he's been saying some very wild things to George. The prop-room's a positive nest of intrigue.'

'Thing is,' Desmond reasoned, 'it would be best coming from you. You're off at the end of the run. We've got the rest of the season to get through. Besides, I gather you've tangled with Potter before.'

'Yes,' admitted O'Hara.

'Not a word in front of John,' warned Dotty.

O'Hara knocked on Meredith's door during the first interval. Apart from a swollen lip Meredith's face was unmarked. Rose was with him.

'Another time,' O'Hara said. 'It was nothing important.'

Meredith came to him when he was changing into his Mr Darling costume for the final scenes.

'Good of you to bother,' O'Hara said. 'It could have waited.' He felt uncomfortable. Now that the moment had come he had no stomach for it. Plastering his face with grease and wiping away Hook's villainous eyebrows, he said what he had to say. Several times he apologised for using what was perhaps the wrong word.

'I'm not a narrow man,' he concluded, 'whatever you might think. God knows, I'm no saint.'

Meredith had remained silent throughout. Now he said, 'It's a wise man who recognises his own sins,' and smiled. He opened the door to leave. 'Before you go down to the nursery,' he said, 'may I remind you that it's a criminal offence to consort with a minor.'

After the curtain call O'Hara waited in the band-room until Freddie Reynalde had played out the audience. Freddie poured a measure of whisky into a coronation mug. 'He's got you there,' he said, when O'Hara had recounted the conversation. 'She is under age.'

'No one can prove anything,' blustered O'Hara. 'She'd be the first to deny it.'

'You've been seen,' Freddie said. 'According to George,

Bunny saw her coming out of your basement. And I shouldn't wonder if Potter hasn't been on his knees peering through the railings.'

'Bunny's a decent man. I doubt if he'd say anything to harm me.' O'Hara's hook caught the rim of the mug. It tipped over, sloshing liquid across the photograph of himself astride a motorcycle. He dried it on his sleeve and said, 'I've a snapshot at home of myself aged ten wearing an Eton collar. It could be her.'

'You're obsessed,' Freddie told him. He wanted to take O'Hara to the Beaux Arts Club to drink him into sleep.

O'Hara refused. They both knew why. 'I can't help it,' O'Hara argued. 'I just feel she's a part of me.'

He was writing a letter when Stella tapped at the window. He wasn't, after all, immediately pleased to see her. He was a little tired of coaxing her into being friendly. Talking to her was like hacking a way through a jungle.

'Is your father all right?' he asked. 'Is it a sprain or a break?'

'I haven't been home,' she said. 'And he isn't my father.'

She was vitriolic about Geoffrey. She couldn't understand how he dared to show his face after what he had done to Mr Potter. Why, he was boasting about it in the prop-room. And after the curtain call, when he was going upstairs to the extras' dressing-room and had bumped into Mr Potter—she wasn't talking at second-hand but had actually witnessed the scene—far from showing remorse he had confronted him as though he was going to head-butt him for the second time. Mr Potter had flinched. His monocle had plopped from his eye.

'Geoffrey has his reasons,' said O'Hara. 'You don't know the full story.'

'He's unbalanced,' asserted Stella. 'He was drummed out of Sandhurst for shooting somebody.'

'Don't talk rot.'

She flared up, shouting that Geoffrey came from the privileged classes. He was a protected species. Mr Potter was a wronged man, a victim.

'You're speaking through your hat,' he said. 'Potter's spent the last fifteen years harming people like Geoffrey. Hilary was eighteen when Meredith picked him up at the BBC Club.'

'Him . . . ?' she said, her face blank.

'He never stood a chance. And there's been a string of others. Why do you suppose he got thrown out of Windsor?'

'You're just jealous of him.'

He laughed.

She told him she was going and she wouldn't be coming back. Not ever. 'Thank you for having me,' she said, grotesquely enough. She had tears in her eyes.

'For God's sake,' he cried, exasperated, and was relieved when she left, slamming the door behind her. He had his letter to finish. Yet ten minutes later he felt he had treated her unkindly and regretted not having gone after her. Perhaps tomorrow, before the matinee performance, she would go with him to the news-theatre for a sandwich. She liked going there. He'd open up his heart to her, explain how much he cared. Trouble was, she'd probably refuse to go unless he trapped her into it. If he called at her house in the morning on the pretext of enquiring after Mr Bradshaw and asked her straight out, in front of her mother, to walk with him to the theatre, she'd have to accept. It would look odd otherwise.

He was pacing back and forth, mulling over what he would say to her, when the biology student knocked at his door for the loan of a shilling for the gas-meter. He was so damned humble that O'Hara was obliged to offer him a cup of coffee. Afterwards he slept badly, his mind swilling with nightmares. He was drowning in the lagoon, sinking beneath the ticking belly of the crocodile.

At midday he walked to the Aber House Hotel and rang the bell. A woman appeared in the area below holding a dustpan and brush. She asked what he was selling. 'My name's O'Hara,' he said. 'I'm from the theatre. I'm anxious to know how Mr Bradshaw is.' He was down the basement steps before Lily could stop him. Flustered, she let him in.

Vernon was sitting in his armchair by the fire, his injured ankle propped on a telephone book. He hadn't shaved and was at a disadvantage.

'Nice of you to call,' he said. 'Bring a chair to the fire.' Hastily he popped in his teeth.

'It's not broken, is it?' asked O'Hara, studing the swollen foot.

'Merely a sprain,' said Vernon. 'I shall be as right as rain in no time.' He turned to tell Lily to put the kettle on, but she had fled into the scullery to tidy herself up.

O'Hara was looking around the room, trying to see the imprint of Stella. He longed to know which chair she sat in, what space she occupied. He noticed the picture frames on the mantelpiece had been turned to the wall. Then he saw her shoes, scuffed with mud, placed together on a sheet of newspaper at the hearth, and his heart leapt.

'It was my own fault, you know,' Vernon told him. 'I wasn't watching where I was putting my feet. It's Mr Potter I feel sorry for. Our Stella says the lad who butted him comes from a well-to-do family.'

'So I believe,' said O'Hara.

'She thinks he ought to be given the sack, but Mr Potter won't hear of it. He told me this morning that he thought the boy had been working too hard.'

'Potter's been here this morning?'

'You've just missed him,' said Vernon. 'Like you, he was bothered about my injury. But that's the sort of man he is, isn't he? One of nature's gentlemen. He's been very kind to me and Lily, as regards putting our minds at rest about Stella. She's secretive, you see. She always has been, and me and Lily get worried about what she might get up to. Don't misunderstand me . . . she's a good girl and generous-hearted once you get to know her. Of course, you won't know her very well, you being a newcomer.'

'No,' O'Hara said. 'I haven't been here very long. I suppose Stella told you I took over from Richard St Ives.'

'She didn't tell us. Mr Potter did. Stella never tells us anything, or anybody else for that matter. She seems outgoing enough but she keeps things locked inside her. That was why I wanted her to go on the stage . . . to help get them out.'

'I would have thought she's very close to her mother,' O'Hara said. 'She's always telephoning her, even if she's only just left the house.'

'She's having you on,' said Vernon. He looked at O'Hara with something like reproach. 'She can't ring her mother.'

O'Hara remained silent. He had the curious feeling that the whole house had fallen silent too, as though listening.

'Lily,' called Vernon, 'Lily, get in here.' He tried to stand up and fell back with a little snort of pain.

'What's up?' demanded Lily. She'd powdered her face and put on a dab of lipstick. It had made her look older.

'Stella's been ringing somebody,' Vernon said. 'Two or three times a day.'

'Not as much as that,' O'Hara said.

'She's told *him* she's ringing her mother.'

'She can't be,' Lily said, not looking at O'Hara. She began to tidy the room. She picked up the shoes from the hearth and put them under the table.

'Who the blazes is she ringing then?' shouted Vernon. Suddenly he thumped the arm of his chair with his fist, remembering all the times he'd caught Stella on the stairs in the middle of the night, staring at the telephone. He asked O'Hara, 'Has she told you anything else about her mother?'

'Only about the rose on her pillow at Christmas . . . with the pearls.'

Vernon and Lily exchanged glances. If anything Vernon seemed more easy in his mind. 'I'd be very grateful, Mr O'Hara,' he said, 'if you tried to find out, discreetly, of course, who she's calling. I have my reasons for asking. It's not just nosiness by any means. I've as much respect for her privacy as the next man.'

'She can't be ringing her mother,' said Lily. 'She doesn't know where she is. None of us do, except she's in America somewhere.'

Vernon fumbled with several beginnings. He wanted to confide in O'Hara, to get him on their side, but he didn't want every Tom, Dick and Harry knowing their business. It wasn't a story that put anyone in a good light. Under different circumstances he would have preferred to cover things over, the illegiti macy for one. It didn't reflect well on Lily and him that they'd thrown Renée out.

'We jumped through hoops to make allowances,' he said. 'I mean, we took her in when she came back from London with her tail between her legs, and we fed her and gave her a roof over her head, but she was forever dolling herself up and going out. She stayed out all night on more than one occasion.'

'She was young,' Lily said. 'She wanted a bit of life.' She was making the excuses to Vernon, not O'Hara.

'She came back again when the baby was born and for a few months she tried, I'll give her that. But she had some daft ideas about this place. She was always trying to turn it into something it wasn't. The upshot was she got herself a room in a house full of artists around the corner. The place was filthy and the neighbours were always complaining.'

'She found herself a job as a telephonist at the GPO,' Lily said. 'She did quite well . . .'

'She won that competition,' said Vernon. 'There were thousands of entries.'

Lily put the shoes on a piece of newspaper on the table and began to pick the mud from them. She said, 'I wanted Renée to leave Stella with us.'

'She wouldn't countenance it,' Vernon said. 'Then we heard she'd lost her job and was up to her old tricks, going out to dances and things.'

'But we didn't know she was leaving the child on her own,' cried Lily. 'We never thought she'd do that.'

'No,' he agreed. 'We never thought she'd do that.'

That was why it had been such a shock when the neighbours came round to tell Lily the baby was screaming and there was nobody answering the door or any lights on in the house. He had to break a window in the basement to get in. The place stank of paraffin and turpentine and dry rot. He wrinkled his nose as if the smell was still in his nostrils. She was in a cot in the back room with a row of night-lights set along the floor. The daft thing was there was a rose on her pillow. It was withered, of course.

O'Hara had risen and gone to stand at the mantelpiece. From time to time he had nodded politely. Now he drummed his finger on the edge of the shelf; he looked bored.

'There could have been a fire,' said Lily. She came to the hearth, worried lest O'Hara should get his hands dirty. She began to turn the pictures round and flap at the mantelpiece with a duster.

'Life is full of conflagrations,' O'Hara said. 'We can never be sure when we'll be consumed by the past.'

She nodded. He had a lovely way of talking, but then, he was an actor.

When O'Hara had gone Vernon hobbled upstairs to ring Harcourt. 'They've all been round,' he said, after telling Harcourt of his accident. 'That director chap came and a couple of the actors . . . the leading ones.'

'I thought you weren't going to the match.'

'Ah, well,' said Vernon, 'Stella insisted. I didn't like to let her down. She was very upset when I fell over. She cradled my head, you know.'

'That was decent,' said Harcourt.

'I told this O'Hara fellow about her mother this morning. I had to. Something's cropped up. He's going to keep an eye open.'

'It's nothing serious, I hope.'

'Nothing me and Lily can't handle. She's been telling her fibs again.'

'Like mother, like daughter,' said Harcourt unwisely.

'Renée wasn't all bad,' snapped Vernon. 'She had a spark, if you remember. She won that competition to be the speaking clock out of the whole of England.'

'The girl with the golden voice,' said Harcourt, by way of apology.

Vernon told him how he had been taken home from the football field in a chauffeur-driven car. He said it had smelt like a bar parlour.

*

O'Hara rode his motor-cycle to the Pier Head and parked it against the granite bollards at the entrance to the Albert

Dock. He waited until the policeman disappeared inside his prefabricated hut before dodging under the railings and walking rapidly away across the giant crazy paving towards the blitzed warehouses. He had some notion of hiding in the ruins until it was time to go to the theatre. He wanted to howl like a dog and hear the echoes all around him.

Crossing the swing-bridge above the water he lost his footing on a streak of black oil. Falling, he struck the back of his skull hard on the edge of the bridge. He swung his head from side to side, trying to get rid of that image of the girl he had known as Stella Maris holding a baby in her arms.

*

There was a crocodile of children winding halfway round the square for the afternoon matinee. George told Stella that St Aloysius's orphanage had a block-booking. The seats had been paid for by the City Corporation. It was a gesture made every year.

She was talking to Prue in the wardrobe—it was Geoffrey's turn to call the half hour, when Bunny came running up the stairs. He wanted to know if she had seen O'Hara. 'Why me?' she said.

'Stop playing funny buggers,' he shouted. 'O'Hara isn't in his dressing-room.'

At the quarter hour, when O'Hara still hadn't arrived, Rose called a taxi and sent Bunny up to Percy Street. The biology student opened the door. He hadn't seen O'Hara all morning because he'd slept in. 'His bike's not there,' he said helpfully, having gone up into the street to look.

O'Hara's bed was made and the dishes washed. Bunny read the unfinished letter on the table:

> It may be that you think my association with a certain person will prevent me from doing anything about Geoffrey. If this is so, you are mistaken. My concern, as on a *previous* occasion, is for a young man whose life may well be ruined by your attentions. I was approached once before, and have been so again. If the situation continues I will have no other recourse than to set the facts before Rose Lipman. It is . . .'

Bunny burned the letter in the sink and sluiced the ashes under the tap.

*

The curtain had to be delayed while Meredith made up as Mr Darling. None of the clothes fitted. He was taller than O'Hara, and thinner. Rose made a front-of-curtain speech begging the audience's indulgence.

The police arrived during the beginning of Act Four, set in 'the hole under the ground'. Tigerlily's braves had finished chanting their ugh, ugh, wah, and Wendy, having reminded Peter to change his flannels and left his medicine bottle perched in the fork of a tree, had flown away home. Babs, emerging into the corridor, saw Bunny sitting on the bottom step of the stairs, being spoken to by an officer of the law. Bunny was smiling in a peculiar way, eyebrows raised as though preparing his face to respond to the punch line of a smutty joke.

Babs said, 'Bunny, what's happened? Is it bad news?',

but he flapped his hand at her in a dismissive gesture as if she had no right to be there.

Stella heard about O'Hara from the child playing Slightly.

'Captain Hook's downed hisself in the river,' he babbled.

Presently, Tinkerbell drank the medicine intended for Peter. It was an affecting moment. *'Why Tink,'* cried Peter, *'it was poisoned and you drank it to save my life. Tink, dear, Tink, are you dying?'*

Stella's hands were trembling as she held the torch. She could hear Mary Deare droning on: *'Her light is going faint, and if it goes out that means she is dead. Her voice is so low I can scarcely hear what she is saying. She says—she says she thinks she could get well again if children believed in fairies. Say quickly that you believe. If you believe, clap your hands.'*

Stella dropped the torch and let it roll into the wings as the children brought their palms together to save Tinkerbell. The light swished from the back-cloth. For a moment the clapping continued, rose in volume, then died raggedly away, replaced by a tumult of weeping . . .

A MAN WITH A WHITE MUFFLER WOUND ABOUT his throat rolled from the black shadows of the Ice Warehouse and the girl stopped and spoke to him. 'I need to make a telephone call,' she said, 'and I haven't any money. Someone's died.'

The man stared at her; he was holding a bouquet of flowers in a twist of paper. 'I wasn't to blame,' the girl said. 'He was happy. He kept saying well done. I'm not old enough to shoulder the blame. Not all of it.'

'Give over,' he said. 'There's no need to make a meal of it.' He gave her five pennies and a farthing and lurched away under the bouncing lime trees, one hand unbuttoning his fly, the other arm raised fastidiously above his head, clutching that bedraggled fistful of winter daffodils.

She rang the familiar combination of numbers. 'It's been awful,' she said. 'There was a man who seduced me.'

'The time,' mother intoned, 'is 6.45 and 40 seconds precisely.'

'It wasn't my fault,' Stella shouted. 'I'll know how to behave next time. I'm learning. I'm just bending down to tie a shoe-lace. Everyone is just waiting round the corner.'

'The time,' pretty mother said, 'is 6.47 and 20 seconds precisely.'